MIDDLE SCHOOL IS NO
PLACE FOR MAGIC

Middle School is No Place for Magic

MIMI OLSON

Middle School Is No Place For Magic

Copyright © 2023 by Melissa Cunningham

All rights reserved. This book or any portion thereof may not be reproduced or used in any manner whatsoever without the express written permission of the author, except for the use of brief quotations embodied in critical reviews and certain other noncommercial uses permitted by copyright law.

Fifth Avenue Press is a locally focused and publicly owned publishing imprint of the Ann Arbor District Library. It is dedicated to supporting the local writing community by promoting the production of original fiction, nonfiction, and poetry written for children, teens, and adults.

Printed in the United States of America

First Printing 2023

Cover Design: Jenny Zemanek
Layout: Ann Arbor District Library
Editor: Michelle Giorlando

ISBN: 978-1-956697-15-5 (Paperback); 978-1-956697-16-2 (Ebook)

Fifth Avenue Press
343 S Fifth Ave.
Ann Arbor, MI 48104
fifthavenue.press

To my daughter, Leah, who brings magic into my life every, single day. This story is for any young person who dreams of trying something new and has the courage to follow through.

1
SPOILER ALERT

Sometimes, I wish I could disappear for real. Poof – and I'm transported to Pinball Pete's Arcade or, better yet, Cedar Point or Universal Studios. No such luck!

How am I going to explain what I did the night my mom left? I guess I'm lucky the school didn't call the police on me. Dad said they could have, for destruction of property. I'll admit it was a stupid thing to do. Problem is, I have NO IDEA what I was thinking when I did it.

I sit on one of the chairs inside the principal's office while my dad walks up to the school secretary, Mrs. Rudolph. I put my earbuds in, open Spotify, and put on my favorites playlist. When I have my earbuds in, I have this game I like to play, trying to read people's lips, but Dad and Mrs. Rudolph aren't turned the right way, so I have no idea what they're talking about. Then, Mrs. Rudolph points to a flyer hanging on the wall behind her.

I glance at the flyer. '**Barrington's First Thanksgiving Talent Show, Wednesday, Nov. 25th.**' *When did they decide to have a talent show?* I quickly take my earbuds out.

"Talent show?" my dad asks. And Mrs. Rudolph starts telling him ALL about how great it's going to be.

"Dad, how long are we going to be here?" I ask, trying to distract him. He's getting excited, waves me off, and keeps chatting it up with Mrs. Rudolph. *Watch, I think, he's going to see if we can perform at the talent show now.* I know how his brain works.

Lately, when I get nervous, even when I'm only a little anxious, my fingertips will get tingly, like they're asleep. I take a couple deep breaths and reach into my pocket for the die I keep in there. I touch the single dot and then add whatever dot I randomly touch next and so on, until my fingers stop tingling. It's a trick I came up with a long time ago when I first started performing. It helps with my nerves.

I glance down the hall and am glad to see Principal Evans booking it toward us. She always walks like there's a fire in the building – super fast and on a mission.

"Hey there, kiddo," she says. Usually she's very chipper, but I can see she's in a serious mood. That doesn't exactly bode well for me, I think.

I lift my hand up in a wave. My dad stands up straight and sticks his hand out, apparently not paying attention to how super-human fast she's walking. His hand clips her stomach, right under her left breast.

NOOOO! I scream, in silence, of course, in my head.

I look at Principal Evans and then at my dad. His face is turning bright red. Principal Evans pretends she didn't notice, breezes past, and waves for my dad and me to follow her.

I've never been called down to a principal's office for doing something wrong. Some kids get their names called out over the intercom so many times, and you'd think they'd won a $100 gift card to Game Stop. They get up, all macho, and practically run out of the room. I didn't want anyone calling my name over the intercom, having to do the walk of shame in front of everyone. I'm not exactly what you'd call 'macho.'

MIDDLE SCHOOL IS NO PLACE FOR MAGIC

Principal Evans's office is bigger than I imagined. There's a gray leather couch across from her desk. Pictures of her family and groups of students hang on the walls. She also has a Dick Tracy comic framed, and Space Adventures, Wonder Woman, Archie. I look around and notice she has tons of comic stuff.

"You like comics, Jay?" she asks, motioning for us to sit on the couch. Then, she smiles at me and waits.

"Mostly Marvel," I say, nodding. "But those are cool."

"Oldies but goodies, right? I fell in love with comics when I was seven," she says. "I made it all the way to the age of seven without learning to read. I didn't care to learn because I had an older sister who loved to read to me. Why bother, you know?"

I nod again.

"I used to love Space Adventures," Dad adds.

"That's how they tricked me into learning. My teacher told my parents to make my sister stop reading to me. Then my teacher told them to buy several of my favorite comics and have them laying around the house. That one right there, Space Adventures, was one. And it worked. Turned out I'd been learning all along and just needed that little push."

"Very cool story," my dad says. "Is that why you went into education?"

She nods. Then, she sits and waits for us to talk.

I don't like complete silence. I'm starting to sweat, so I'm glad when my dad starts talking. I really want to get this over with and get out of her office before anyone sees us and starts asking questions.

"Well, I'll start by saying that I think Jay owes you an apology, for sure, and he needs to apologize to the whole garden club. But I wanted to explain a bit, you know, about what's going on in... in our family," Dad starts. I stare at him for a minute. I don't think I've ever seen my dad this nervous, not even the night we performed at the Michigan Theater.

3

"Oh?" she says, tilting her head. "Is everything all right? I hope it's nothing worrisome."

"It's really not. Well, it is kind of a big change, but it's nothing terribly serious, or even permanent."

SPIT IT OUT! I want to scream.

"It's my wife, Beth. She was accepted into a university in Iowa for poetry, to get her master's. So, it is good news, in a sense."

"The Iowa Writer's Workshop? Wow, that's impressive. I didn't even know Beth was a poet."

Neither did I, I think. *Not really.* I knew my mom had this habit of stopping whatever she was doing, pulling out her notebook and jotting stuff down. I remember her going off to poetry readings and that kind of thing. Does that make her an actual poet?

I watch my dad to see how he reacts to Principal Evans's comment.

"Yes," Dad continues. "She's been writing poetry her whole life. But we only learned that she was going to Iowa about six weeks ago. It's been a hard, kind of a fast, move."

Principal Evans has this way of peering into your soul when she's thinking. I reach into my pocket for the die. She takes a few seconds to respond, and then says, "One of the friends I made when I was working on my master's degree in business was married and had two kids who lived in another state. I remember it was hard for all of them, but they made it through."

"We will, too," Dad says, super quick, and then glances at me. "We're not separated or anything." There's another pause.

I'm reeling, and I can feel my cheeks turn red. *Why, Dad, why?! Why would you tell my principal all this private stuff about our family?!* I feel like I'm one of those metal ducks in the water gun game at the carnival, and Dad's humiliating comments are the stream of shooting water knocking me off-kilter. And he keeps on spraying me right in the face.

"The night Jay did that damage to the school garden, well, that was the day his mom left."

Damage... more like destroyed the garden, I think. He's downplaying it a bit, and that's why I can never stay mad at my dad. Now, I feel guilty that he feels like he has to go to bat for me like this.

"I can assure you he will not do anything like that again." Dad's eyes dart to mine and I nod. He looks back at the principal. "Beth's only going to be gone for 18 months... 24 at most."

Again, he looks at me with his worried eyes. I look over at the principal. She is nodding and kind of smiling. Then, she looks at me and says, "Well, that explains a lot. I know it's out of character for you to do something like that, Jay. That's a lot of change without much warning. As happy as you must be for your mom, you must be missing her, huh?" I don't know what it is about Principal Evans, but when she looks at you like that, you cave.

I nod. "Yup," I tell her. Dad winces. He reaches over and squeezes my shoulder, like someone's died or something.

"It's OK, though," I say, quickly, trying to sound normal while scooting away. "It's not that big of a deal. She'll be home for Thanksgiving. It's fine." Now there's a lump in my throat. I swallow hard and keep going. "I am sorry for kicking that garbage can over and pulling out those plants." I sigh.

I can still see my dad's face when I told him what I did and, even worse, when we walked down to the school late that night and he saw what I'd done. I never want to see him that disappointed in me again. Mom knows about it, but we haven't talked about it. I don't plan to, either. It feels like I might start crying. They both look at me, staring for a minute. I blink a few times.

"What can he do to make up for this," Dad asks, "aside from apologizing?"

Principal Evans looks out her window for a few seconds, which seem like an eternity. "Well, I think spending some time helping our custodians clean up the yard. That would be a good start. I'll let them know you'll be coming up here to help in the next few days, Jay. I also want you to reach out to Mr. Zimmerman to see what plants you'll need to replace and work with him on getting that done. It's totally understandable that you were going through some strong emotions that night but it's never, ever acceptable to damage school property. You know that don't you?"

I nod my head. Dad pipes up, "That sounds good. And he will pay for the plants in the spring with the money he earns from our shows."

"That'll be fine," Principal Evans says. "Thanks for letting me know about your family's transition. Jay, you should let your teachers know. It's good to let them know what's going on at home. I'm here, if you ever need to talk to someone, and so is Mr. Durham." She looks at my dad and says, "He's an excellent school counselor. We're so fortunate to have him."

So, now people think I need therapy? I'm *not* going to talk with Mr. Durham about my family problems. Mr. Durham is also the eighth-grade basketball coach and I've been secretly practicing all summer to try out for the team. I'm not going to say anything to make him think I can't handle stuff.

"Thanks so much, Principal Evans. I really appreciate this," Dad says, then quickly turns to me, expecting something, I can tell. What does he want to me say?

"Um, yeah, thanks," I say.

Principal Evans stands up, so we do, too. We're nearly out the door when she drops the bomb.

"Oh, wait a minute. Did you hear we're having a talent show this year? We would love for the two of you to be in it, if you're not busy that day. It's the 25th of November, right before Thanksgiving break. If you'd be willing, we could have you finish out the show with your magic act. It would be such a treat for the kids!"

No, it wouldn't, I think. *Say something, doofus. Say anything! Why do I always go blank at times like this?*

"Mrs. Rudolph was telling me about that," Dad says. "I didn't know if you'd want a parent-son duo in the show. I understand if it's only for the kids."

"I think it should be only students," I manage to blurt out.

"No, not at all. I think it'd be fantastic," says Principal Evans. My dad's face lights up in a big smile. "I mean, you wouldn't be in the competition, being professional magicians, but I think it would be great to have you perform as the finale. It's Jay's last year here in middle school and, all this time, none of us have seen you two perform. I'd really love to see your act. From what I hear, you're both quite talented."

"Well, OK then, that sounds great!" Dad says and turns to me, grinning, happier than I've seen him in weeks. "If it's the 25th, your mom will be home. She'll be able to come, Jay. Won't that be cool?"

I feel like a rabbit frozen in fear. My fingers are buzzing. I don't answer. I'm up to number 327 in my die count.

"Jay..." Dad says. "You OK, bud?"

"Yup," I say, walking as quickly as I can.

"See you on the first day of school, Jay," Principal Evans says. "I'll have one of the custodians call you about meeting up for the schoolyard cleaning before the end of the week. Monday will be here before we know it!"

"Thanks," I say over my shoulder. I just want to get to the car.

* * *

ON THE DRIVE HOME, Dad starts plotting out the trick sequence we could do for the talent show. He's going to be talking about the stupid show now until it's over. At least he's not bugging me about the trash can I kicked over or the stupid school garden.

I know I shouldn't have done it. It was my bad luck one of the custodians saw me. Or maybe it was good luck because I'd only yanked out half of my mom's plants when I heard him shouting at me. My mom started the middle school garden with a few other parents who pushed the school to create one, and she'd made me work in the garden for two years straight.

I would have pulled them all out if he hadn't stopped me, mid-rampage.

* * *

DAD BLATHERS on about the talent show the whole drive home. "How about we add in a few more callouts? You know, get more audience participation. I know, we can do the Spelling Bee! We haven't pulled that one out in a while."

I look over at him to see if he's joking. Nope, he's staring straight ahead at the road, completely serious. How can he think it's a good idea to ask an audience of middle schoolers to shout out words that we have to then incorporate into our trick? Does he not know what kind of words kids my age love to say? Sometimes, my dad can be so naïve.

"Dad, please, no. The kids don't want to participate in the magic show. Let's not have any audience participation."

He looks at me and shrugs, chuckling. "You're probably right about that one," he says.

I ask if I can wear a mask during the talent show. Dad stops laughing. "You know as well as I do that a big part of the act is facial expression, so I don't think adding a mask to our get-up is a good idea."

"Do we have to wear the capes?" I try for a small win. I will not be wearing the cape.

Dad looks over at me like I asked him to swallow a bee. "What's a magic act without a top hat, bowtie, and cape? That's always been our trademark look."

Trying to get my dad to change anything in our act, unless it's his idea, is nearly impossible. That's why I'm burned out. It's the same costume, the same tricks, the same facial expressions, over and over…UGH!

I reach into my pocket and start turning the die in my hand. I run through a few different scenarios, thinking about what could happen if we go through with it:

1. The very best case: Dad and I get through our magic act without me becoming the laughingstock of Barrington Middle School.
2. Mediocre bad: I get a nickname out of the show that's even worse than my current nickname, which I hate: Magic Jay.
3. Worst case: Something goes terribly wrong; my dad trips and steps on our bunny, can't find the crimp cards, the flash paper sets the stage on fire, or Dad gets flustered by the hecklers. And trust me, there will be heckling. Can you imagine performing a magic show, with your dad, in front of an auditorium full of sixth, seventh, and eighth graders?

2
THE MAGIC CIRCLE

What I've always liked about magic is that you can learn pretty much any magic trick if you are good at following directions and practice enough. The key is practicing.

I was five when I learned my first magic trick. It was a simple ball and cup trick. The ball and cup trick dates to Ancient Egypt, something like 2,500 B.C. Magicians have taken those routines and made them better and more spectacular since then. It's kind of mind-blowing, if you think about it. Penn and Teller once did the ball and cup trick using clear cups. They were able to do the trick so fast no one could figure it out. That is the ultimate, to me. Still, they ended up getting kicked out of the Magic Castle nightclub for breaking one of the cardinal magicians' rules: *Never (and I mean ever) reveal the mechanics behind your trick to the audience.*

My dad is particularly good at sleight-of-hand tricks. He used to do the ball and cup trick using baby chicks. It was amazing until people started asking him how the chicks felt about being shuffled around under cups. My dad told me, secretly, that he'd never thought much about how the chicks felt. In any case, he stopped doing it after that.

We still use our bunny in our act, but we're very careful. Mabel's one spoiled rabbit. We pretty much treat her like a cat. She's litter trained so she can wander our house all day. She only goes in her cage at night.

For three years, from the time I was five until I was eight years old, I was obsessed about learning magic tricks. I watched my dad's and other magicians' videos on YouTube. By the time I did my first show with my dad, I'd mastered spoon-bending and I could make a coin disappear five different ways. I got especially good at card tricks. Dad calls me his mini-cardician.

That was five years ago. Now that I'm 13 and starting my last year at Barrington in exactly four days and 16 hours, I've made the decision that I do NOT want to be my dad's sidekick anymore. I *especially* don't want to perform in front of my entire school. I've tried to keep my school and show life separate. Very few people at Barrington even know I'm a magician. That might be because very few people know who I am, but that's beside the point. Thinking about the talent show makes me sweat, which makes my armpits itch, which makes me irritated.

I wish I could think of some way to tell my dad that I'm sick of our shows without hurting his feelings. He's been so depressed about my mom leaving. I'm worried how he'd react if I suddenly quit on him. I shouldn't have pretended to be fine this last year. My parents have no idea how unhappy I've been. It makes me so angry, thinking about how my mom gets to bail and how I'm stuck. How is that fair?

* * *

My phone dings right as I put some leftover chili on the stove. It's Anthony, one of my three best friends.

> Just got done registering bro, next year is gonna be epic we're at the top of the food chain now

I ignore it, set the phone down and start grating some cheese up for the chili. Ding. Then a few seconds later, three more. I wipe my hands off on a piece of paper towel. He's texted:

> What's up?

> You there bro

I have to answer, or he'll keep pestering.

> I'm here but I'm not hyped for going back to school

> Why you down did something happen

> Sort of...

> Calling a crew meeting we need to compare schedules, anyways

Anthony loves being the one to call the crew meetings. We tease him by calling him the drama king. He'll call a meeting for any silly reason, like if one of us saw a good movie or we're planning out our summer camps. The meetings are always at Lamar's.

Then, it all started to make sense when, the other day, Anthony confided in me that he has a crush on Lydia, Lamar's twin sister. I caught him staring at her in the mushiest way when she came down to kick us out of their rec room. I guess I can see it. Lydia had a bit of a glow-up over the summer. But... *gross.* She is way too much of a sister to me.

> Bro it's not that big a deal

> Well, what is it then

I don't want to get into it texting. I still can't believe my dad said yes to us doing the middle school talent show. What is he thinking?!?!

Actually, I know what he's thinking. Money is tight now, with everything that happened over the summer and my mom in college. He thinks that the talent show will make the kids want to book us for their birthday parties and stuff. But middle schoolers don't think magic is cool.

UGH! It's useless. Dad is convinced this is going to be good advertising for our birthday party shows. He can't see how weird this is going to be, especially for me. Nothing I say is gonna change his mind. I'll have to come up with an ingenious plan to get out of the show. Maybe I do need the crew to help me think of something. Anthony texts:

> Meet at 8?

> K

Then, a group text comes in:

> Mt at 8 & you know the place

I really hope he doesn't spray himself in that awful cologne.

* * *

WE ALL LIVE within a five-block radius of each other, and Lamar's house is pretty much in the middle. My house is the smallest. We have a three-bedroom ranch. Lamar's house is the largest, by far, and he lives closer to downtown by about three blocks. Both of his parents are doctors. He has a big bedroom with a couch and bean bag chairs, so we usually end up hanging out at his place. Plus, his mom always makes sure we have good food to snack on. She knows I like fruit and she'll wash up some grapes and apples for me. Plus, Lamar's mom lets us call her Dee.

I walk in and grab an apple from the fruit bowl and head up to Lamar's room. I'm the last one to get there. Anthony and Sal are arm wrestling when I walk in. I slump down on the bed.

"So, what's up?" Lamar asks. "Why do you look so down, Jay? Did you hear something about your mom?"

Lamar's blunt like that. He always cuts to the chase.

"No, it's nothing to do with her."

An image of my mom pops in my head from the last time I saw her. My stomach tightens. Lamar nods his head and throws a knowing glance my way. He's the one I share the most with about my parents and their 'split' or whatever you call it.

"What then? Did you find out Claire's going out with someone else?" Lamar asks.

"No, it's not about Claire," I say, fibbing a bit. I admit part of what's embarrassing is thinking about performing in the talent show in front of my ex-girlfriend.

Sal reaches over me to grab the bag of Doritos from Anthony. "Hey, save some of those for the rest of us!" he says.

"So…" I start, waiting for Sal and Anthony to stop fighting over the chips. "Did any of you hear about the talent show the school's planning around Thanksgiving?"

"The one at Langdon Elementary?"

"No, there's one planned for Barrington this year, too. My dad caught wind of it, and he wants us to do our act."

At first, none of them react. They stare at me like a trio of blank-faced emojis.

I try not to be frustrated. "Guys," I say, slowly, "My dad

wants me and him, the two of us, to perform our show, like, in front of the whole school."

Anthony's eyes get wider. He talks with his mouth full of Doritos. "Dude, how did your dad even find out about that? You know how he is. You should have hidden that from him at all costs. What were you thinking?"

"I didn't tell him about it! First, it was Mrs. Rudolph. Then, the principal suggested it to him. She said we could be the finale!"

Sal sighs and kind of rolls his eyes. "So, your dad wants to enter the talent show with you? What's the big deal?"

Anthony glares at Sal. "Dude," he practically yells. "We're in eighth grade. We're top dogs at school this year. This is OUR year. Jay doesn't want to look like a clown. And stop rolling your eyes. It's getting on my nerves!"

Sal throws up his hands, rolling his eyes. "Whatever. I don't think it's that bad of an idea."

Anthony punches him in the arm. When Sal ignores him, Anthony looks at me and says, "I get it, bro. I mean, I don't want to be a jerk but you and your dad's act… I mean, it's good and I know I don't know a lot about magic but not, like, Criss Angel good. You know what I mean? Now that would be a different story."

He didn't have to tell me that. I know our act is fine for kids' birthday parties and even the county fair, but we aren't doing Carbonaro-level tricks.

"That's why I've got to find a way out of it, no matter what."

They all stare at me for a second. Anthony claps his hands together. "I got it. I'll pull the fire alarm. Right before you go onstage."

"You'd do that for me?"

"Of course. I'd take the hit."

"I would, too," Sal quickly adds.

"Ok, I might have to take you up on that, guys, but only if there are no other options."

Sal, always Mr. Cautious, chimes in. "On the other hand, you could look at it another way. I've always been jealous of you getting to be in your dad's act. I mean, my dad's hobby is genealogy and I have to listen to boring stories about my way-dead relatives all the time. I always thought it was really cool, you getting to do magic together. I mean, look at what you can do. This might be your chance to shine. Maybe show off to Claire. That card trick you learned over the summer is cool. What's it called again?"

"The Four Burglars? That's a pretty easy one, actually."

"See, you think it's easy. It's really cool!"

"Yeah, but is your dad gonna make you do the thing where you float on that fake-looking, raggedy old magic carpet?" Anthony asks.

"We *always* do the levitation trick."

"No. Just no. That is not gonna be cool in eighth grade. And what about the thing where you disappear and reappear in that gold glittery box he built?"

"Probably." I start sweating again.

Anthony gets up and starts to mime while he talks. "OK, so picture this. Your dad opens the super glittery box and there you are, standing there like a dope, the whole school staring at you. You're up there in front of the whole school wearing a red and white striped cape and sparkly red bowtie. I mean, think about that."

Sal socks Anthony in the thigh. I close my eyes and sink back onto Lamar's bed. Anthony hits Sal in the arm.

"Look," Anthony says, "I'm not trying to be mean. It's up to us homies to keep it real. I'd want the truth if I were being forced to be in a kiddie magic show at my school. I mean, did you see Marcus? He has a bushier beard now than my Uncle Ted's. I'm not kidding."

"So what?" Sal slumps into a bean bag. "Who cares? Wasn't it you who says we shouldn't give a crap what other people think? Huh, Anthony?"

"I know what I said, but this is the reality our bro is facing. Look, it's not only the fully bearded dudes and the jocks. It's the ladies, too. Think about all the hotties who'll be sitting in the bleachers. Sure, they might think Mabel is cute. What girl doesn't think a fuzzy white bunny is cute? But they sure as hell won't think Magic Jay is cute. Not in that getup he wears. The show's meant for little kids, not grown kids like us. And what's to say his dad won't make him do it next year, in high school. I mean, where will it end? It has to stop at some point!"

I sit up and take a deep breath. "Lamar, you've been really quiet. What do you think?"

Lamar starts pacing. "So, I don't think it's going to be as bad as Anthony's making it out, but I guess I can see what he means. The thing that really sucks is that you've been wanting to get out of those gigs for a while now. I know you don't want to bum your dad out with everything else going on, but you might have to tell him. Just be blunt about it."

Anthony comes over and puts his arm around my shoulder. "Look," he says, "if you can't get out of the show by talking reason to your dad, we'll think of a way to get you out of this."

He looks at Lamar and Sal. "That's what friends do and that's what we gonna do. We'll put together a foolproof plan. You know what? I think we need to meet every day until we figure this thing out." Our drama king sits there, grinning like the Cheshire cat.

3
DIRTY TRICKS

For the first few seconds after I wake up and smell pancakes and bacon cooking, I feel happy, like a heavy blanket has been lifted off.

"Pancakes are ready," my dad yells up the stairs. "Jay, Jenna, first day of school. Time to get up, sleepyheads."

Instantly, like some witch is casting a dark spell over me, I feel heavy again as it dawns on me that my mom is halfway across the country. She's the one who always made us pancakes and bacon on the first day of school. This is the first first-day-of-school she is going to miss in my whole entire life.

Before my mom was accepted to some university in Iowa for her poetry writing, (*really, poetry?!*) I thought there was some kind of age limit on going to college. I mean, going back to college at 44 years old seems pretty weird to me. Plus, who wants to go to school to learn about poetry? And leaving your whole life and family... I never thought she'd be able to do it. I kept thinking she'd change her mind right up to the day she drove off. Even after that, I kept thinking she'd come back and say it was all a big mistake, that she hated Iowa, but that was three and a half weeks ago.

MIDDLE SCHOOL IS NO PLACE FOR MAGIC

When we Zoom, she looks happier than I've ever seen her. She started wearing makeup and doing something different with her hair. She never used to do anything like that, and I think she looks ridiculous.

My mom always had a way of sensing what I was thinking, like some mom mind-reading trick. But that seems to be gone now, too. She rambles on and on and asks me a ton of questions, but it all feels superficial. I used to love talking with her but now it's annoying. She is annoying. So, I sit there with a fake smile on my face, and I wonder if she can tell that talking to her is literally the last thing I want to do. I wonder if knowing that would wipe that happy grin off her face.

"Jayster, it's time to get up kiddo," my dad yells up the stairs again. He sounds edgy. I take a deep breath and throw the covers off.

Mom took us clothes shopping before she left. First, I try on my new jeans and my new Schrute Farms t-shirt – Dad and I love *The Office*. I decide both the shirt and jeans look too new and end up throwing on some cargo shorts and my dad's old Radiohead t-shirt.

"There he is!" Dad says, trying to sound chipper when I walk into the kitchen. He's setting out some pancakes. Jen reaches past me to grab one with her fingers.

"Hey, use your fork," I tell her, pretending I might stab her with mine. She giggles.

"Do either of you know how to get straight A's?" Dad asks. I groan. He says the same joke every year.

"By using a ruler!" Jen shouts. I shake my head.

Before we leave, Dad hands us each $5 and says we can get a snack at the gas station on our way home.

"Do you need me to drop Jen off?" I ask.

"No, I want to go today, meet her teacher and stuff. But if you could pick her up, that'd be great. You'll have to wait a bit but maybe you could do some homework at the picnic table?"

"We won't have homework on the first day, Dad. At least, we better not. I'll wait for her, though. No problem."

"Thanks, bud," he says and pats me on the back.

"No worries," I say, standing up and giving him a quick hug. "I'm gonna take off, then, and meet the guys. Have a good first day, Jen, OK? Come right out after school's done and I'll be by the front sign."

"Ok, bye, Jay!" she says.

* * *

AFTER WE MEET UP, I walk into the school building with my crew. We enter the hall for eighth graders, and I head to my locker at the far end. On the way, I pass Claire, who is talking with her group of friends. Sal nudges me in the arm. Thank goodness she doesn't seem to notice us or, at least, is pretending not to.

I see her smile at her friends. She must have gotten her braces off during the summer. Her teeth, which used to be kind of crooked, look perfect now. I notice she's wearing shiny pink lip gloss. *Don't sweat, don't sweat.* I will myself to take control of my armpits and focus on opening my locker.

We almost kissed once. It was the last day of seventh grade, which seems like eons ago. We'd been dating for a few weeks at that point. Plus, we'd been friends since the middle of sixth grade. Claire was my first girlfriend and, to be honest, I had no clue what I was doing. She bent in for a kiss and I backed up. I kind of freaked out, and I totally regret it now. The next day, Claire dumped me. I texted her ten times, trying to explain that I was surprised. I didn't mean to embarrass her. Claire ignored all my texts. I haven't talked to her since that day.

I thought about that near-kiss, over and over, all summer long. I can feel my cheeks turning red as I open my locker, thinking about Claire's bright pink lips and her new, perfect smile. I wish I could go back in time.

"You OK?" Anthony asks, walking up. We have first hour together.

"Sure, why?" I check my shirt for sweat stains. Clear for now. As I close my locker, Anthony puts his hand on my shoulder.

"Remember, bro, I'm always gonna keep it real. You need to keep reminding yourself that Claire doesn't like you. She ignored all the texts you sent to her after you two nearly kissed," he blurts out. "She totally blew you off and she doesn't deserve a stand-up guy like you!"

"Shhh!" I hiss, glancing down the hall. To my relief, she and her friends had walked off.

"Ok, ok," he whispers. "I'm just sayin,' she ignored all the texts you sent over the summer. I mean no reply. Nada. I get it; she was your 'first love,'" he says, using air quotes, "but she's history now. She's not worth the time of day. Time to move on."

We walk into first hour. I can't believe he's still talking. Sometimes, Anthony can be clueless. And, considering he has NEVER had a girlfriend, he really likes to give me love advice. I know he doesn't mean anything by it, though. He's trying to be a good friend.

"Anthony, come on," I whisper and shoot him a look. He nods and mouths the word 'sorry.' Coming from anybody but Anthony, I might have slapped a dude for saying all of that.

But I know he's right. Claire isn't my girlfriend anymore. She isn't even my friend. I wonder now if I ever knew her at all. I doubt she even knows about my mom taking off. I try not to let it, but that part really bothers me. Claire had been one of my closest friends pretty much all through middle school. Then, as soon as we nearly kiss, she goes MIA? And, today, she doesn't even act like she knows me?!

Thankfully, it turns out Claire isn't in any of my classes. That's one bonus of going to a big school. And it was a good day, all in all. I like most of my teachers. The only one who gets on my nerves is my English teacher, Mrs. Milton. She has that mega coffee breath you can smell all the way from the front of the room to the back, and she's way too excited about Shakespeare and other old writers. She talks nonstop. Some teachers act so lonely, it kind of makes me sad. Other than that, and having to see Claire in the hallway now and then, it wasn't half bad.

4
BALABREGE AND THE FLAMING MOTHS

"Hey, bud, how was your day?" Dad asks as soon as I let myself and Jen into the house. I'm surprised to see him. He normally comes home from work around 5 o'clock and it's only 3:45.

"Pretty good," I say. "Why are you home?"

"Daddy!" Jen yells and throws herself at him for a hug.

"I left early. I wanted to surprise you and Jen for your first day back to school. Your grandpa's coming for dinner. Going to make tacos tonight, your favorite," he says. I notice the grocery bags on the counter.

"Did you get anything good to snack on?" I root around in one of the bags.

He takes out a bag of Cheetos and tosses it to me.

"Cool, thanks, Dad!"

He motions with his eyes for me to sit down at the table. While he puts the groceries away, I tell him about how the biology teacher said he likes my Radiohead t-shirt and that they're his favorite band, too. I even tell him about Mrs. Milton and non-stop talking with that horrible breath of hers, which makes Dad laugh. It's nice to see his eyes light up.

"Overall, I guess it was pretty good for the first day," I say. "How was your day?"

"Good!" he says. "I'm sure your mom is going to be happy to hear about your day. She called earlier and she's been thinking about you and Jen all day. She's going to Zoom in to talk with you in about 15 minutes. She wants to make sure she got a chance to talk to you alone and then she'll Zoom with Jen. Sound OK?"

"I can't, sorry," I lie before I can stop myself.

Dad looks at me funny, wiping some Cheetos powder off his fingers with the dishrag. "You have someplace you urgently need to be?" he asks, sarcastically.

"Yeah, I told Lamar I'd be over right after dropping off my backpack. And I'm already late." I look at my phone for emphasis.

Dad puts down the dishrag and turns to give me his full attention over the kitchen bar. His quizzical look quickly turns to confusion.

"Jay, come on," he says. "Not tonight."

"Yeah, Jay, stay home with us!" Jen chimes in. Boy, that's unhelpful. I give her a quick glare.

"I came home early and we're having tacos around 6 o'clock. I want you to talk to your mom. I also want to talk to you about the talent show. I'm excited. Aren't you?"

I lean my chair back and roll my eyes.

"What's that look about?" Dad asks, angrily.

Now, I glare at him. "You know what? If Mom wanted to see how my first day of school went, she could have been here." I stand up, grab a banana from the fruit bowl and head toward the back door.

"Jay, you better stop right there," Dad says, following me out to the back porch. I keep walking, heading toward the shortcut through my neighbor's yard.

"Jay!" Dad says loudly. "Please don't walk away angry. It's

fine. I'll tell her you'll Zoom when you get home. I want you home no later than 5:30 and it's after 4 now. You hear me?"

Dad's been giving in a lot more since my mom left. In a way, that also makes me sad. I turn back toward him before disappearing behind our neighbor's garage.

"Yup, all right," I say, throwing my hand up.

He waves back but his face is tight. I can tell he's stressed. I feel bad. It isn't exactly his fault my mom left. I know they fought a lot, especially the last year. Mom was always getting angry with him for all the money we spent on our magic shows and all the time he was away doing the magic shows, going to magic conventions and all that stuff.

I can't help but feel better getting away from him, though. I don't feel like talking to anyone. Instead of going to Lamar's, I head toward a little patch of woods a few blocks away. It was part of a riverbed once that used to run through our neighborhood. Houses couldn't be built in certain parts of our neighborhood because of the deep gully. Now, us kids have taken over those areas.

I enter the trail and run down the steep hill to the grassy open area at the bottom. In Miller Woods, you'd never know you were in a city neighborhood. A couple of years back, my crew teamed up with some of the older kids in the neighborhood to build a huge fort-like structure out of long logs that had fallen in the woods. We filled in the gaps in the logs with hundreds of sticks.

This is the first time I've been down there in about a year. I have to admit our fort looks a lot smaller to me than when we first built it. I scrunch down low to get in. The inside of the fort is always littered with cigarette butts and old beer cans. The stoners like to hang out down here after dark.

I have the woods to myself for about fifteen minutes before a mom brings her three screaming kids down the path to run around. It reminds me about the times I'd come down here with my mom. I wonder what she thought when I wasn't there to Zoom with her. She probably felt hurt, but I have no intention of Zooming her later.

My dad refuses to understand how much it bothers me that my mom gets to do whatever she wants, no matter the consequences. She's such a hypocrite! She was the one always talking to me and Jen about choices and consequences. Seriously, that was her big thing.

"Think about your choices," she'd say. "Every choice has a consequence."

We even have a family saying: "Don't be a Balabrega."

Balabrega was this Swedish magician from the late 1800s who used the wrong fire accelerant for his trick and literally blew himself and his assistant to pieces.

"Well, maybe your consequence is that you don't get to Zoom with me whenever you feel like it," I mutter to myself, pulling some sticks out of the fort and breaking them into little bits. I throw them on the ground. "Not everything is about you, Mom," I say a little louder. Apparently, I startled the mom who finally sees me through the branches of the fort. She peeks into the opening but keeps walking, calling for her kids to hurry it up.

I climb out of the fort and head the other way, back up the trail that leads out to the neighborhood. She turns to glance at me, and it seems like she looks relieved to see me go.

On the way home, I think, *you know, I do a lot of the stuff my parents ask. I help them out with Jen. I practice for the shows because it makes my dad happy. I get nearly all A's. I think I've been a pretty good kid, all in all.*

I decide right then that I'm not going to give in and Zoom with my mom. Maybe not forever but for one whole week, even if it means fighting with my dad. Mom was right, there are consequences to the choices you make in life.

5
THE DISAPPEARING ACT

The day my mom told us she was leaving was one of the worst days of my life. My head was pounding, so I went to my room right after she made her 'big, exciting announcement.' Not long after that, Jen knocked and asked if she could snuggle. I had a feeling it was going to get bad between my parents, so I let her climb into my bed. I gave her my good headphones and turned on some electronic music I knew she liked. They started fighting. I mean, I'd heard my parents fight before, but this was way, way worse. I guess my dad was as surprised by Mom's news as I was.

"How do you expect us to pay for this, Beth?" I heard my dad say, practically shouting, which wasn't like him. "My God, we're already in debt up to our ears. I know how much a master's degree costs, especially for out-of-state tuition. Come on, Beth, do you really think we can afford that right now? I mean, it could be as much as 50 grand by the time you're done. Let's be realistic."

Either there was a long pause or Mom was talking so low I couldn't hear her, at first. Jen was wiggle-dancing around and snapping her fingers to the beat, making it extra hard to hear. I swear my mom said something like, "Maybe it won't be your problem to deal with at all."

Dad said, loud and clear, "What did you say to me?"

I heard my mom shushing him, whispering about not wanting us to hear them fighting. "Half of the tuition is covered by a scholarship. I'll be able to get a job teaching in a college after I graduate. It's only 18 months," she said, in a low voice. "I'm sorry if you think that's selfish but a lot of couples make this choice and if you can't support me– "

"I would have been a lot more supportive if you hadn't blindsided me," Dad said. "You knew this was in the works for months and you hid it. And by some couples, you mean Gabe and Rebecca? 'Cause I'm pretty sure they're getting a divorce."

I remember my stomach burning after he said the word 'divorce.' I took out my die and started adding, but I quickly lost track of the numbers. I was too distracted. I must have looked upset because Jen ripped off her headphones and demanded to know what was going on. I put my fingers to my lips to keep her quiet. I didn't hear anything for a few seconds and then my mom spoke.

"Jimmy, I swear I didn't intend to blindside you. You can look at the acceptance letter if you'd like. It's dated less than a week ago. Iowa has one of the best master's programs for poetry. Truthfully, I didn't tell anyone I was applying because I didn't think I'd get in."

Now Dad was quiet. They were talking so low that I couldn't hear anything after that.

Jen looked confused. "It's OK," I whispered, motioning for her to put the headphones back on. I smiled at Jen and gave her a thumbs up, pretending like everything was OK. Then, I shut my eyes so she wouldn't pick up on anything and pretended to be falling to sleep.

"Jimmy?" I heard my mom say, worried. "It's only 18 months."

"I thought you were happy, relatively speaking," Dad said. "I feel like a fool, a real fool."

There was a long silence after that. Then, I heard my mom walk toward their room, which is next to mine. I heard their door click shut. My dad left, slamming the kitchen door on his way out. So that's how we learned my mom was leaving us for 18 months to get her master's in poetry out in Iowa, of all places.

The next morning, after breakfast, they sat Jen and I down to tell us they were sorry if we heard them fighting and that everything was going to be all right. I was glad Jen was oblivious. Dad said we all needed to band together and support Mom because she was fulfilling a lifelong dream, but he said it half-heartedly. Mom promised to visit at Thanksgiving and Christmas, plus spring break. We're going to Iowa for a couple weeks next summer, I guess. They told us they were going to stay together, but I think that's iffy. I know what I heard.

6
HAT-TRICK

Dad and I drive in silence, out of the city, past the strip malls, out to the suburbs of Ann Arbor. He's upset that I refused to Zoom with Mom all week, so we drive past the high-end thrift store, the Wendy's and into a fancy neighborhood called Foxberry Estates without saying a word to each other.

I know most of the kids my age who live in Foxberry because the whole neighborhood is bussed into town to Langdon Elementary and Barrington Middle School. The houses in Foxberry are huge, at least to me.

Quite a few are already decorated for Halloween. A lot of my friends come out to Foxberry to trick or treat because they give out the full-size candy bars. I wonder if the crew will even go trick or treating this year now that we're in eighth grade. It makes me sad to think I'll never be able to trick or treat again. When we're talking again, I'll have to ask my dad what he thinks about us going out one last time.

We pull up to a house with a big blow-up Charlie Brown. I used to think those blow-ups were so cool. Now I know what they cost and it's crazy to me that anyone would pay a hundred bucks for a big balloon.

I hate doing shows where kids might know me. I pray it'll be a young crowd, and no one will recognize me.

No such luck! I see her as soon as I walk in the door. Gini is in my grade at Barrington. In fact, we've been going to school together since kindergarten. She smiles when I walk in and waves a little. Instantly, my pits are wet.

I follow Dad in, his red cape flowing behind him. He likes to walk into a venue with a flourish. I try to hide behind him, to fade into the room.

After he makes his grand entrance, squirting a couple of kids with his flower corsage, we go back out to the van, carry in our trunk and the rest of our equipment, and set up.

"You better get ready," Dad whispers. "Where's your uniform? I hope you didn't leave it at home!"

"It's in my duffle," I say, pointing to the bag.

"Great." He rolls his eyes. "It's probably wrinkly. You should have hung it up."

I grunt and grab the bag. I *wish* I'd forgotten the uniform at home.

Gini is standing near the kitchen door.

"Where's your restroom?" I ask, my face turning red thinking about her seeing me in my show suit with the red cape and top hat. I mean, it's fine to dress in a stupid top hat and cape when you're 40 and all your friends are old and weird, too. But here I am, going through this humiliation in front of one of the most popular girls in school.

Gini hangs out with a big group of girls who live in Foxberry Estates. FBE girls, we call them. One time, I got stuck doing a science project with two FBE girls. They spent the whole time talking about all the designer clothes they were going to buy when they were old enough. I'm not even kidding. It was the most boring conversation I've ever been forced to listen to.

In the bathroom, I throw on my outfit and look at myself in the mirror, feeling like a total dork. My phone dings and I glance at the message. It's Anthony, texting that he's come up with a list of the top 10 ways to get me out of the Thanksgiving talent show. Of course, he wants the crew to meet later to talk it over.

> K, tx, text later. At show

I send the message to Anthony and then peek my head out of the bathroom door. Quickly, I scan the house to see if Gini's invited any of her friends over. I know she has a little brother. I spot him, the birthday kid, a short, round-cheeked boy with a perma-grin on his face. No other eighth graders, thank God! It is a full house, though, and Gini's mother introduces me and my dad around to everyone. Gini must have had 20 cousins there, or at least that's how they were introduced.

All the women are dressed in colorful saris. A few have red dots on their foreheads, which means they're Hindu and married. That's the kind of stuff you learn at Heritage Night, which they have every year at Langdon. Dad is part French but only, like, a quarter. He jokes every year that we should set up an info table about France during Heritage Night and cook French fries. He thinks it's the most hilarious idea ever.

Hindus are interesting to me. They believe everyone has this third eye, like an inner eye, which can help you focus on God. That's another reason they wear the red dot, as a reminder to keep God in your thoughts. I always thought that was cool, and I liked Gini's Heritage Night table the best. Every year, about 30 of Gini's friends and family set up henna stations and a huge table full of Indian food. It smells so good! Mom was teaching me how to cook Indian food before she left. The last dish we made together was tandoori chicken. I spot some on the kitchen counter. There must be 20 different dishes lined up. Gini's mom catches me eyeballing the food.

"Please, Jay, make a plate and eat," she says, trying to get me to take a plate. "If you are not in a hurry, we are not in a hurry. Take your time. I know growing boys need their nourishment!"

"Thank you so much for the invite," Dad intercepts. "We might grab something to eat after we're done with the show. It sure does look and smell delicious!"

Gini's mom smiles up at him. "Please do eat after the show." She turns to look around and then yells, "Ragini, where are you, dear?"

"Coming, Mother," I hear her say and then she appears in the kitchen doorway, a quizzical look on her face.

"Ragini, please gather everyone in the living room. You are ready?"

Dad nods. "Yupper-doodles – all set!"

Let the embarrassment begin! I think.

Gini stares at my dad, wide-eyed, like he's a three-horned alien. Then, she starts going up to different groups of people, asking them to head to the living room. I notice Gini's dressed in jeans and a sweater that has the words "Rock Star" written on it in cursive, not in a sari. Gini seems like one of the nicer FBE girls but she's quiet, especially around boys. I can't remember ever talking with her much besides stuff like, "Hey, what did the teacher say about today's homework?"

My dad transforms into someone completely different when he's doing magic. Once we start the show, it's like this super joyful guy comes out. It's not fake, either. I can see a cloud lifting off him. His face lights up. He lives for this stuff. I wish I still felt that way.

I feel calmer as the show goes on, though, and we run through our itinerary. It's a pretty good crowd for a house show. Lots of oohs and ahhs and laughter. They're really into it. Gini even looks like she's enjoying herself. I'm starting to feel pretty good, actually.

For the last part of the act, I have to get Mabel out of her cage, which is hidden under the tablecloth. We always have two volunteers come up for this last act in the show. Of course, Dad picks the chubby-cheeked birthday kid. Then he calls Gini up to the front. I meant to tell Dad *not* to pick her. Just my luck! I take a deep breath. *A few more minutes and we'll be done*, I tell myself.

My dad and I do a series of scarf tricks first. We call them 'silk effects.' Gini and her brother are participating, and it's going fine. Gini is smiling and her brother is giggling the whole time. My dad is hamming it up, like he does, telling one corny joke after another. The kids are going crazy, laughing and jostling each other.

Finally, we're ready for the finale which involves Mabel. Mabel has done the show for five years, so I'm not too worried. I'm already thinking about the chicken tandoori. Then, right as Dad hands Mabel to Gini, Mabel starts pooping.

Plunk, plunk. Two pellets fall onto the fancy living room rug. I see it happening, but Dad doesn't. He's busy explaining what we're going to do next.

Gini stands there, her eyes wide. A poop pellet lands right in her hand as she takes Mabel. Her expression goes from smiling to disgusted.

"Gross!" she yelps and shakes the pellet off her hand. It lands onto the fancy rug. Now there are three bunny turds on the floor. All the kids sitting cross-legged in the front row see this. They're shrieking and laughing. Dad looks confused but keeps going. I wonder if I should pick the poop pellets up with one of the silks. Instead, I stand there frozen.

Gini is holding Mabel at arm's length and looking right into my eyes. Her cheeks are getting more and more red by the second.

Are those tears in her eyes?

OMG!

I quickly walk over to take Mabel from Gini, both for Gini's sake and for Mabel's, who likes to be held tight to my chest. I can see she's scared.

Dad still doesn't know what's going on. He steps right onto a pellet when he walks toward me. The kids shriek. Gini looks like she wants to run, but she stays put, staring at her hand. I doubt there's anything on it. Bunny poop is pretty solid. But it still sucks to be pooped on. I know this from firsthand experience.

Mabel has never pooped during a show. *Maybe it's her age*, I think, stroking her forehead the way she likes. She's trembling, poor thing. She is getting old.

Then it dawns on me that it's my fault. I'd forgotten to take her out before the show. That's part of my job, to make sure she goes right before we start.

My dad is looking even more confused. He still doesn't know he's stepped on the pellet and is walking around their ornate rug. I look at Gini's mom and she has a horror-stricken look on her face. I bet the rug is worth a ton of money. I want to hide, but I know I have to say something.

"Dad," I say, trying to whisper. "Mabel pooped and it's on your shoe."

He looks surprised and stops dead in his tracks. I'm not sure how we're going to save the act. I have this utter sinking feeling in my gut.

Dad doesn't skip a beat. He slips both shoes off and says, "Yikes! Looks like we need a clean-up in aisle four. So sorry about that! Working with live animals can be a gamble."

Gini's mother is super nice about it. "Don't worry one bit. We will clean up after. Please go on with the show!" She starts clapping and then everyone joins in, even the kids.

Dad takes Mabel from me, and I rush to pick up the pellets

with one of the silks. I look at Gini and she's smiling at me, a little. I feel like THE biggest loser.

Right after the last trick, I am gone, heading back to the bathroom as quickly as I can walk through the crowd. Usually, we both stay up front and I hold Mabel so the kids can pet her. I'm sure my dad has that confused look on his face again, but I don't turn to check. I'm still holding the silk handkerchief full of bunny poop.

The bathroom door is locked. I turn, nearly running into Gini's mom.

"There's another bathroom upstairs, dear," she says. "Go on up. It's to the left."

I thank her and she tells me what a marvelous time everyone had. I mumble thanks, again, and jog up the stairs.

7
DO YOU BELIEVE IN MAGIC
(IN A YOUNG GIRL'S HEART)?

I run up the stairs and find the bathroom. I close the door, throw out the bunny poop, and try to open the window.

Something is happening. I have a strange feeling, like the walls are closing in. I want to run outside into the fresh air, but I can't face anyone yet, not breathing hard the way I am. Everyone will think I'm a maniac.

I go out into the hallway and sink down onto the floor. I'm feeling slightly dizzy, so I put my head into my arms. My chest feels tight and I'm kind of scared. I've never felt like this before, like it's hard to get a deep breath.

"Hello?"

I don't want to look up. I already know it's Gini.

Maybe, I think, *if I ignore her, she'll leave me alone.* But she doesn't. She stands there and starts walking down the hall toward me until I can see her wriggling her toes in her sparkly silver sandals. Finally, I look up. I wonder if she's mad about Mabel, but she's sort of smiling.

I raise my eyebrows, something I learned to do recently, kind of a jerky gesture meaning, "Yeah? What do you want?"

"It's OK," she says. "I wasn't really that grossed out by what happened. I'm sorry I said 'gross.' Then, all the kids started laughing and–"

"You're sorry?" I interrupt, not meaning to. "I'm the one who should be sorry."

"It's fine." She shrugs her skinny shoulders, staring down at me.

I'm surprised. I thought she'd be texting all her friends by now, telling them what happened, dishing on me. Instead, *she's* apologizing? I stare up at her and don't even know what to say.

"Can I sit?" she asks. I nod and she sinks down next to me, leaning against the wall. We sit like that for a few seconds. It feels like an excruciatingly long time. I'm trying to breathe like a normal person. Then, I start sweating again. My mind is reeling, trying to think of something to say. Right when I was about to ask about her cousins, she asks if I like doing magic.

"Sometimes," I tell her. "I used to like it more, when I was younger." I surprise myself by being so honest. Something, about the way she's looking at me, her brown eyes and thick eyelashes, makes me feel a little more relaxed. It feels like she really wants to know, like, it's not only small talk.

"What about now?" she asks.

I sigh. "Sometimes, I feel really stupid doing the magic shows, especially in front of people from school." My stomach clenches and, suddenly, I get this weird lump in my throat. Gini doesn't seem to notice.

"I could tell," she says, grinning. I've never noticed her braces before. She has silver and gold bands on that made her look like she has a lot of cavities. I'm pretty sure that's not what she's going for. She has a nice smile, though, and very pretty pink lips, I notice. *Is that lip gloss?* I wonder what flavor it tastes like and, for a second, wonder what it would be like to kiss her. Then, instantly, I feel bad for thinking that way. Why does my brain always have to go there?

"I know how you feel," she says. "I hated dancing in front of everyone at Heritage Night. Now all the moms want me and my cousins to dance at the Thanksgiving talent show. Did you know there's a talent show this year? It's the same thing with piano. I love playing the piano, but I HATE recitals. I feel like I'm going to throw up every time I have to give a recital. I ask my mother; why can't I simply enjoy playing the piano? Like, isn't that good enough? But, of course, she doesn't listen. She tells me I'm being silly, that I should be proud of my so-called talent. It's not talent, it's that I like playing, so I practice a lot."

I nod, shocked that she's talking so much. I like listening to her. I feel my breathing slow down. I start to feel less dizzy.

"Panic attack," she says, randomly.

"What?"

"What you were having when I first came up here; it could be a panic attack. My older brother used to get them, especially before big tests. I remember my mother teaching him about meditation. Have you ever tried it?"

I shake my head no. She tells me to sit like her, legs criss-crossed, back straight.

"Now see how your hands are all balled up? Go like this," she says, putting her hands on her knees, palms-up. I feel silly, but I do it. She smiles.

"Now close your eyes," she tells me.

"Um, OK?" I really hope this isn't some kind of trick to make me look even more idiotic. I peek for a second to make sure she's not recording me. Her eyes are closed.

"Now take a few deep breaths," she tells me. "In and out. Breathe with your chest, not your stomach. Don't think of anything but breathing."

As I sit there, a sadness comes over me. I feel myself tearing up. I don't want to risk crying, so I open my eyes, blinking fast. I watch her breathing. I feel a little sneaky, spying on her that way, but not bad enough to stop.

Gini is wearing a dark purple headband in her straight black hair. It pulls her hair back from her face and, up close, I can see that she has a tiny divot at the end of her nose and a small roundish scar at one temple. I'd never noticed that before, or that her skin is so smooth. She has dangly gold butterfly earrings that shimmer every time she takes a breath. I try not to look at her chest breathing. I stare at her lips. The lower one sticks out slightly farther than the top.

My heart starts pounding again, only in a good way this time. I think about how strange it is that we've gone to school together – even had the same teachers a couple of those years – and I've never really looked at her before this.

Gini used to wear her hair in braids every day. *Didn't she also have glasses?* I remember thinking she was smart. I knew she was good at playing the piano, but I never knew that she was really into it. Most of my friends are forced to take music lessons. I never had time, with the shows, and I was always kind of jealous. But they all grumbled about it. None of them liked their music lessons.

Suddenly, Gini opens her eyes, startling me out of my trance. She looks straight at me, and her eyes are friendly, even kind of happy.

Is she flirting with me? The thought races through my mind, and it gives me butterflies, for a second.

"Feel better?" she asks.

"Yeah, much, thanks," I mutter, wiping my sweaty hands on my jeans.

Gini look down at her hands. "You probably think my family's weird, huh?"

"What? Why would you think that?"

"I don't know," she says, and suddenly, she is acting like the shy girl I know from school.

"I think you're lucky," I tell her. It made her smile a little, again.

"Why?"

"I mean, look at this house and all the family and friends you have." Right then, we hear an eruption of laughter drifting up to the second-floor landing. I can hear my dad's booming voice in the mix. I look at her, like, *see what I mean?*

"Yeah, I guess you're right."

"At my house, it's usually only me, my sister, my dad..." I say, blushing. I almost add my mom. "I don't know if you heard but my mom moved to another state. She's getting her master's degree. But she's coming back, I think..." I quickly add. I'm shocked at how easy it is to talk to Gini. I never open up like this to girls.

Gini nods. "I heard about that," she says. I look away and we sit in silence for a minute.

"I suppose you're right," she says. "I should feel lucky. But, sometimes, I feel different from my friends, you know?"

I nod, but honestly, I have no idea what she means. Why does she feel different? I was about to ask when her mom calls up the stairs.

"Gini, are you up there, dear?"

She rolls her eyes and I laugh under my breath. She puts her finger up to her lips to gesture for me to stay quiet. We hear her mom walk away from the stairs, asking people if they've seen Gini.

"I have to go," she tells me in a quiet voice. "But I'm wondering..." she pauses, looking me right in the eyes.

"What?" I thought she was going to say something about my mom again.

"Do you want to be friends? I mean, not only acquaintance friends, which I feel like we've always been, but real friends?"

I'm sure I look totally bug-eyed. I nod and swallow hard. "I mean, yeah, that would be cool," I say.

She looks genuinely happy which makes me feel a little lightheaded again.

"I'm going to get my phone. Stay here." She runs down the

hall and into a bedroom at the far end, then comes back a few seconds later holding a phone in a glittery purple case.

"Quick, what's your number so I can text you?"

I tell her and she types it in. Her fingers are long and slender, I notice, which is perfect for playing the piano. I'm tempted to tell her that, but instead, grin at her when she looks up.

"There, I sent you a message. Don't read it until you get in the car, OK? I'm gonna Snapchat you, too, if that's OK?"

I nod. God, I feel like an idiot who can hardly talk. *Pull it together!*

"That sounds good," I manage. "Hey, thanks for coming up here and talking to me." *Ugh, lame. Who says 'hey' when they're talking to a pretty girl? And 'thanks for talking to me?'*

Gini reaches her hand out to help me stand up. I'm a little startled but let her take my hand. I'm even more startled when she keeps holding my hand for a few seconds. Then, her hand slips away and she turns, giggling a little, to walk down the stairs. I guess Gini isn't as shy as I thought she was!

8

HYPNOTIZED

As soon as I buckle my seatbelt, I read her text. She's sent a link to a song and wrote:

> Music for meditating. See you soon!

She'd added a smiling emoji with two red hearts for eyes. I put my headphones on and start to listen to the song. Dad motions for me to take them off.

"What happened back there?" Dad asks, angrily. "Where'd you go? You didn't even grab a bite to eat. Lucky for you, Gini's mom sent us home with leftovers."

"I forgot to take Mabel out." I glance up at the house.

Dad pushes the ignition button but sits there for a few seconds.

"Jay, you gotta learn to role with the punches. Messing up is part of being an artist."

"OK," I say. "Can we go?"

He stares straight ahead, his lips pursed. I know he's getting ready for some kind of lecture. I can feel the blood rushing to my face. I hate fighting with him, hate this tension we keep having lately.

He turns to me, won't let it go. "What do I always say? No show is the same and no show is perfect. We're always going to have little mess-ups–"

"Yup, you're right, Dad," I say, interrupting him. I don't want him sugar-coating things. I'm sick of that, too. He sits there, our SUV running in front of Gini's house. I hope she isn't watching because I feel like I might lose it.

"We recovered pretty well, didn't we?" he asks in his softer voice.

"Lucky Mabel didn't piss all over everything," I say, knowing that will rile him up. Why am I being such a jerk lately?

"Hey! Watch the language." Dad takes a deep breath.

"Sorry," I say quickly. "Can we go, already?" I really want to go.

"So, Mabel pooped a little. You have to lighten up, bud. Come on," he says, punching me lightly in the shoulder. "Everyone laughed! But taking off like you did, before we even took a bow, that wasn't cool. Or professional. I turn around to see if you want to do one last trick and you're gone. I mean, was it that embarrassing to you?"

"I don't want to talk about it right now," I plead. "I want to go home."

Dad strums his index fingers on the steering wheel. He looks irritated, but he puts the car in drive and starts off down Gini's street. I'm hoping we're done talking. No. Such. Luck.

"Look, Jay, I know this is a tough time for our family but we're gonna work it out. Your mom and I have always worked things out and we will do it again."

I can tell in the tight way his face looks that he doesn't believe what he's saying, not fully.

"Can we not talk about that, either?" I ask, staring out the window.

"Just one more thing, your mom is Zooming you tonight. She's getting really worried about you. You haven't talked to her all week. You need to," he says.

"I'll see how I feel, Dad," I say, looking straight ahead. "All right?"

He takes a deep breath. "Fine, I can't hog-tie you to the chair, but I hope you decide to talk to her. Punishing her isn't going to help anyone, least of all you."

We pull up to a stop sign and I can feel him looking at me. I ignore it. He turns on NPR and I stare out the window as we pass the neighborhood club house with the pool and tennis courts. Some older kids I don't recognize are playing basketball on a brand-new court. The court in our neighborhood needs new paint lines and one rim is missing a net.

I was always a little jealous of the FBE kids when I was younger. They had nicer clothes and all the latest technology. Some of the moms brought their kids McDonald's and Subway – walked it right into the lunchroom. Ethan's mom would waltz right in and drop it off to his table, like he was some kind of prince. I was lucky if my mom got around to packing my lunch for me. Mornings are her reading time, she always says.

But now I can see how you'd feel a little stuck being out in a neighborhood in the middle of cornfields, with only the kids who live there to hang out with. You'd see the same faces every time you went for a walk or the pool and, TBH, most of those faces are white. Maybe that's what Gini was talking about when she said she felt different.

It makes me realize how happy I am to live in the city. I rarely see anyone I know when I go downtown. I don't run into familiar people when my friends and I skate to Pinball Pete's or when we're hanging out, people-watching in the University of Michigan Diag, this big, grassy area where the college kids hang out.

I like that feeling, being free. Plus, there are lots of different types of people. It struck me right then, that being different is normal in the city.

Maybe I'll take Gini downtown one of these days. It would be so fun to take her to the café and get a couple of frappes. I imagine us sitting there, laughing and talking the way I'd seen older teenagers hanging out. I bet she'd feel free, if I took her downtown.

"That young girl seems nice," my dad says. *He's fishing,* I think. I swear, sometimes, it's like he can read my mind. I hate it.

"Yeah," I answer. "She's OK."

Dad grins and winks at me, which irritates me even more. *Why is he always getting on my nerves lately?*

"Hey, what did you think of my new joke?"

"What was it again?" I ask.

"What's the difference between a rapper and a magician?"

"What?"

"A magician will disappear, while a rapper will diss-a-peer." He laughs. He always laughs out loud at his own jokes.

"It's bad, Dad," I say. "Like, really bad." He roars with laughter, which makes me laugh.

"Cool, I'll keep it in, then." He gives me a thumbs up and another wink.

Dad takes the back roads into town. We drive along the Huron River. I put my headphones on and start listening to the chill song Gini sent to me.

Dad taps me on the shoulder and points out a tall, white crane sitting near Fuller Bridge. Further down, I see a white-tailed deer munching on the grass in someone's backyard, but I don't mention it. I don't want my dad starting up about the deer cull the city approved last week.

It had been dreary when we drove to Gini's but now the clouds are starting to break apart. Streams of light are shining down through one of the clouds. Mom calls them God rays. She says they makes her feel hopeful.

Thinking about Gini, about us hanging out together, makes me feel lighter. She's right, the music she sent is relaxing. Maybe Mom will come back, and everything will go back to being normal. Maybe Dad will understand that I want to take a break from magic. Maybe I'll get on the basketball team with Lamar. Maybe...

I spread my hands on my legs, palms up, close my eyes, and breathe.

9
CHINESE WATER TORTURE

"Hi Mom," I say with as little cheerfulness as I can muster.

"Jay!" My mom waves through the computer screen, VERY cheerfully. "Oh my goodness! It's so good to see your face!"

"It's only been one week," I say, trying not to roll my eyes.

"I know, I know! But it's been a big week – your first week of your last year in middle school. I can't believe it."

What's not to believe? I think. "Um, yeah, I guess." I'm not sure what my mom wants me to say. Then I notice she looks different. "Did you cut your hair?"

My mom runs her hand through her very short hair. Then, she turns slightly, and I see she's put a streak of bright blue on one side. I groan. I can't help it. I don't think she notices.

"Yeah, I even got a little adventurous. See?" She turns so I can view her blue hair streak full-on. "What do you think?"

"It's, um, cool?" I say.

She laughs, genuinely. "I know, I know. I feel a little silly. I don't know what I was thinking. Should have used the kind I could wash out. Oh well, it'll grow out. So, tell me what's been going on with you. I want to hear all about your week!"

A heavy feeling settles in my chest, and it must show on my face. Mom squints and tilts her head. It's the look she gets when she's worried or upset.

"Or…" she says, "just tell me a few things that happened this week. Dad told me that the two of you are going to be in the middle school talent show."

"Yup." I take a deep breath.

"Well, you know what? I'll be there! It's the day before Thanksgiving break, right? I'll be flying in that Tuesday."

"That's nice."

"Yeah." There was a long pause. "Um…tell me about your teachers."

"They're OK, I guess," I say. I hate that I don't feel like talking to her. I feel like I have this knot in my stomach, again. That's been happening a lot lately. Maybe I'm getting an ulcer. We read about those in health class.

"I have a teacher who sounds exactly like Winnie the Pooh," she says. "It's really distracting trying to digest all the different forms of poetry, acrostic versus landay and all of that, when I'm sitting there dying for him to say the word 'honeypot.' I very badly want him to say it, just once." She runs her hand through her blue streak and laughs, but this time I can tell it's a little forced.

"Do you like your classes?" I ask, throwing my mom a bone. Her face lightens up.

"I really do. I feel like I'm with my people here. I mean," she stops and takes a deep breath. "I didn't mean to say… you, Jen and your dad, you're my main peeps.

I don't say anything, but I nod.

"I only meant that it's good to be with a group of people who are all passionate about reading, writing, critiquing each other's work, trying to grow and get better. There's a lot of energy, you know what I mean?"

"Sure, I get it," I say.

"Do you?" She looks into the camera, straight at me. I see she's starting to tear up. Again. Mom does this nearly every time we Zoom. Seriously, it's the last thing I feel like dealing with right now.

"I have to go." I put my hand to my forehead. "I'm starting to get a headache." It isn't exactly a lie. "I'll get Jen. OK?"

I can see how hurt my mom is, but she puts on a mom smile.

"Well, I hope you had a good first week. Sweetie, you know I love you to pieces, right? I can't wait to come home in November. I know it seems like a long way off. It seems like a long time to me, too. But if we can talk like this more often, it'll fly by in no time. OK, hon?"

I nod. "Jen!" I yell and wave to my mom.

"Love you!" she says, blowing kisses.

"Love you, too," I say, turning to bolt out of the room as Jen comes bounding in.

* * *

BEFORE BED, I walk into Jen's room to bring up the subject of her taking over as Dad's magic show assistant. She's dressed in a bright pink crop top. Her lips are the same shade of pink. Jen is talking into the camera on her phone.

"You making a video, or something?" I ask.

"Well, duh!" she answers. "And thanks for interrupting me." Jen turns and gives me a pouty look. I try not to crack a smile.

"Ok, sorry. Can you pause for a minute?"

Jen slaps her phone down way too hard and looks at me, like, 'well?' She is always going through different stages. Dad says girls her age have a lot of hormones and stuff they're dealing with and that's why Jen can be so moody. Sometimes, all she wants to do is cuddle with me on the couch and watch cartoons. Clearly, she's having a diva moment. I'm going to have to be subtle.

"Check out this new trick I've been working on," I tell her, trying to get her enthusiasm up. I take out a half-dollar coin, hold it up and drop it from one hand into the other. Instantly, the coin levitates back up to my top hand.

"Whoa," Jen says. "How'd you do that? Show me again. I want to see if I can figure it out." This is a good sign.

I do the same trick again. Jen claps. "Pretty cool, bro," she says.

"Did you figure it out?" I ask, a little test.

"Nah, but that's OK."

"Want me to show you?"

"Sure," she says and then she picks up her phone and points it at me.

"Are you recording me?" I ask. "You know I don't want the secret of this trick getting out there."

"Fine," Jen says and puts her phone down. "Go ahead."

"This one took me forever to learn." I pick up the coin and do a classic retention, squeezing the coin into my palm. Then, I pop it up into the air.

"Ouch, that looks like it hurts!" Jen says. "Didn't your hand hurt, practicing it over and over?"

"Yes, it hurt pretty bad at first. You have to keep your hand super still and pop it up by rolling your thumb. Then, I had to learn how to catch it. It was a tough one!"

"Hmm." That's all Jen says before turning back to her mirror and picking up some glittery eye shade stuff. She takes a Q-tip and rubs some on her lids.

"You know," I keep going anyway, taking a seat on her bed. "Being Dad's assistant the way I have been the past five years really has had a lot of perks. I mean, A LOT."

Jen doesn't even blink. *Boy,* I'm really going to have to reel her in.

"Like, you know how we do a lot of parties. There's always cake and ice cream. Plus, when I was younger, at least, I'd usually get a party bag with lots of candy. I'm talking most times. Not to mention all the time I get to spend with Dad. That's irreplaceable, really. I mean, you can't put a price on that kinda bonding, you know? I think that's why Dad trusts me so much and I get lots of freedom." I pause, trying not to look her right in the eyes while trying to figure out if it's working. I feel like I'm trying to sell her a vacuum or something. I remember two other selling points I'd thought of.

"And there's the costumes. I mean, mine is OK, but the assistant costumes they make for girls are the bomb! You like to get dressed up and stuff. You're so good with Mabel, too. I mean, she's really your pet, if you think about it."

I think I've made some genuine points. *I'm going in for the big ask!*

"I guess what I'm saying is, if you want to take over as Dad's assistant, I'd be willing to think it through. I mean, I've had all this time and success, everything that goes into being a magician's assistant. But I am willing to step aside and let you have your turn in the spotlight."

Jen looks at me out of the corner of her eye. I can see a little curl of a smile on her lips. It worked!

"No way, José," she says.

"What? I thought you'd want to at least give it a shot, Jen?"

"No thanks. That's very kind of you, but I'll pass."

OK, now she's being a smarty pants. Jen turns back to the mirror and starts putting purple sparkly eye shadow on.

"You don't want to even give it a try?" I sound desperate.

"I have my own plans. I'm going to be a fashion icon. I've already started my own YouTube channel so I can do a fashion vlog."

"Fashion vlog?" I can't help but start laughing hysterically. I launch myself back on her bed, rolling from side to side. "Like, an influencer?"

Jen leaps up from her chair and pounces on me. I grab her and we roll around, wrestling, until we both crash on the floor.

"Hey! What's going on in there?" Dad yells from the living room.

"We're good!" I say, standing up. Jen is still glaring at me.

"All right, all right already," I say. "I give up. You'll actually probably make a good vlogger." I turn and start to walk out.

"I'm sorry you're stuck being Daddy's assistant," Jen whispers.

"It's OK," I say, and walk out the door. Anthony called it. He told me if Jen liked magic, she'd already be doing it. Onto Plan B, I guess.

10
ZIG ZAG GIRL

I think about Gini the entire weekend, wondering what it will be like seeing her in school. I haven't spilled the beans about our talk to the crew yet. I mean, I'm not about to admit that I have a crush on Gini if she doesn't feel the same way about me.

Monday, I walk into the school thinking she'll be at her locker. She's not there. Gini is in my last hour, math, and I think she's in my lunch period, too. When the bell rings for lunch, I hurry to get to the cafeteria, grab my usual – pepperoni pizza and chocolate milk – and station myself at our table so I can see the other students streaming in.

"Yo, what's up?" Drake walks over. The look on his face is a mix between curious and irritated. I'm in his seat.

Drake is a new friend. He moved to Ann Arbor about a year ago, but only started sitting with the crew at the start of this year. He plays football with Anthony, and he thinks Sal is funnier than all get-out. I see Drake has his usual lunch – a cheeseburger loaded with mayo and pickles, three orders of fries, and two Cokes. Drake's at least a half foot taller than me and already has a six-pack from lifting weights all year.

Anthony is constantly challenging him to arm wrestle. Drake always wins. He wears his hair in dreads and his voice has already dropped. He doesn't put up with any BS, so I know the only way he'll let me stay in his seat is if I'm completely honest about the situation.

"Hey Drake, you mind if I sit here today? I'm trying to scope out the door to see if a girl I like has this lunch period or not. You know what I mean?" I am so embarrassed to be blushing right now and sweating like a pig.

A huge grin spreads across his face and he nods his head knowingly. "I got you," he says, making this clicking sound out of the side of his mouth. He goes to sit across from me right as I spot Gini. Drake follows my eyes to the door. He clicks again and winks.

We both stare at Gini's girl pack as they walk right past us. They are all looking right at me with these sheepish grins on their faces. Gini waves, even, smiling. I literally turn all the way around to make sure she's actually waving at me and not someone sitting behind me. One of her friends giggles and jostles her.

"What's up with that?" Anthony asks. I didn't even notice him walking up to the table. He plops his lunch tray down and sits next to Drake.

"Shhh," I whisper.

"Why you always shushing me?" He reaches across and punches me in the arm.

Lamar and Sal walk up together. Lamar raises one eyebrow, like he's some kind of detective, which makes Sal laugh really loud. Drake starts cracking up. I wait for Drake to spill the beans about Gini. He saw her wave and say hi to me, but he only looks at me with that grin on his face. That's when I know we're actual friends.

"Well, then, you gonna tell us?" Anthony asks. I don't even know what to say. It was one conversation and a text.

"We had a show at Gini's on Saturday for her little brother's birthday and we talked, that's all," I admit, quietly.

"Gini Varma?" Sal asks.

"Show?" Drake asks. "What kinda show?"

Shoot! I think. I was flustered and let it slip. I make it a habit to not talk about the shows at school. Drake's turning out to be all right, though. My crew knows my rule about keeping magic and school separate, so they're all looking at me, waiting to see if I'm going to trust Drake enough to tell him.

"Yeah, so, not a lot of people know and that's the way I like it, but my dad's a magician and I sort of help out with his shows."

Drake looks at me wide-eyed. "Like, you help get the show set up for your dad?" he asks. "Kind of like a roadie? My cousin's been a roadie for the Randy Newman Band for years. That's cool, dude."

For a minute, I consider letting Drake believe that. 'Roadie' sounds a lot cooler than 'magician's assistant,' but he didn't say anything about my crush, so I decide to let him in.

"I'm actually my dad's assistant," I say, keeping my voice low.

Drake doesn't say anything for a second. He sits there, nodding his head. I can see he's taking it in.

"Like, magician's assistant? That's dope!" he finally says. "I saw this guy out on Main Street doing this street magic show. It was cool. Do you ever do that? That wasn't your dad, was it? People were throwing money in his top hat. He was raking it in!"

I smile. This isn't the reaction I was expecting.

"We mainly do kids' birthday party and church events, stuff like that. But, like I said, I don't really like to advertise it."

"I got you," he says, winking and giving me one of the clicks with his mouth again.

"OK, so now that's cleared up, are you going to tell us about

Gini or what?" Anthony asks right as my phone pings. We're allowed to have our phones out at lunch.

It's Gini starting a chat with me.

> Hi Jay!!! I'm staying after school today for Robotics Club. I'm on a team with two seventh graders Aiden and Leah but we can have four people so do you want to join our team?!?!

I look over at her. She turns, talking with a friend. "Is that her?" Sal asks.

> Sure, yeah, that would be fun.

I send it before I can think too much and get nervous. "That was Gini," I tell the gang.

Sal laughs and says, "Go Jay!"

"Get it, boyee!" Drake reaches across the table and gives my shoulder a light smack.

> Great!!! Meet me in the orchestra room after school. I gotta grab my violin before Ms. Chapman locks the door. K?

> Cool. Will do

I want to look over at her table so bad to see if Gini is showing her friends. What if the whole thing is a practical joke and they're all in on it? I couldn't see Gini doing something like that. Then, again, I don't really know her all that well.

"Gini Varma," Anthony says. "I haven't thought about her since fifth grade with Mrs. Sumtner. She always seems so shy. Guess not anymore!" he laughs. "Did she DM you just now?"

I nod, turning the phone to show Anthony and Drake what she wrote.

"Dude," Anthony says, "she asked you out?"

That startles me. "No, I mean..." *Did she?*

"Let me see," Sal says, grabbing the phone. He reads Gini's message with Lamar looking over. Lamar is being quiet about the whole thing.

"Looks like she's asking you out, bro!" Sal says. "I mean Robotics Club isn't exactly the most romantic of dates but she's def trying to hook up with you. I might be a little jealous." Sal grins, handing the phone back.

"Hey Lamar?"

Lamar eyes me, knowingly. "Talk and walk?" he says.

"Yeah, walk with me over to the trash."

We get up and say "see ya" to the guys. I'm relieved when Anthony and Drake start in on Sal about playing football. At least, they're not talking about me and Gini.

I lead Lamar over to the far trash can so I can check out Gini and her table. I try to be sly about it, glancing over. Gini is sitting in the middle of the table, smiling right at me. She must have seen me getting up. The rest of her friends are all talking and laughing with each other, but Gini is sitting there with her pretty, shy smile.

I smile back and I know right then that she hasn't sent the chat as a joke. The invite is real. I also know Lamar has seen all of this and is waiting for me to explain everything, which I do as we walk to fourth hour together. We get there a little early.

"So, that's how it all went down," I say, telling him all the details right up until that minute.

"I like Gini," Lamar says. "She's nice."

"Do you think she's pretty?" I ask him.

"Sure, I guess. Don't ask me that, dude. It's whatever you think that counts. I have different taste."

"Hmm," I nod. I've never heard Lamar mention having a

certain type of girl he likes. The bell was ringing so we'd have to continue *that* talk later.

"Well, thanks for listening," I say, walking into our class.

"Yup. You'll have to tell me how it goes at Robotics. Do you still want to shoot some hoops later? Basketball tryouts are in a month. You have some work to do if you want to make it on the team."

"For sure." That's another thing I still have to tell my parents. I want to be on the basketball team with Lamar this year and in high school. I think Drake might try out, too. Sal has been playing for years. I've been getting better, sneaking in hoops whenever I can. I like how basic basketball is; the rules are simple enough. I can focus 100% on the plays and not worry about anything. It's good for that – blocking out thoughts. It's all about the practice, like doing magic. I'd be so excited to get on a team. But it'll mean missing a lot of our magic shows.

* * *

FIRST THINGS FIRST, before I head into class, I text my dad to tell him I'm staying after for Robotics Club. My normal routine is that I ride my bike to school. Then, after school, I ride to Langdon to wait for Jen to get out. It's a little over half a mile. Then, I walk my bike the other half-mile with Jen to get home. Dad usually gets home two hours after that, unless something happens at work that makes him late. Today, Jen will have to wait half an hour for me. Not that big of a deal, I think. I figure she can hang out on the playground, or something.

I send him the text, but I can't check what he wrote back until after school.

> We will have to talk about this when I get home. I was able to reach Reagan's mom and Jen is going home with them, so you don't need to pick Jen up from school. Just go straight home after the club is over. I'll be home a little early today. See you then, bud.

Yeah, I think, *we will have to talk about it. Since when did I have to be the one responsible for getting Jen home every day? Why does that have to fall on me every day, on top of everything else? I'm not the parent.* Seriously, I feel like swearing.

I type **wth?!?!?!** back to him, right as Gini walks to my locker. Ugh! My cheeks are red again. I quickly backspace to erase the text and shove the phone in my back pocket.

"You OK?" Gini asks.

"Yeah, my dad's being a jerk, that's all." I didn't mean to let that slip.

"Is he upset that you're staying for robotics? I didn't mean to get you in trouble."

"Um, no. It's fine," I lie. "I always have to get Jen from school and walk her home. You'd think I could have a break from that for one day, right?"

"Oh, I didn't know. Is Jen your little sister? I remember seeing her at class parties but I never knew her name. She's such a cutie. I love how bright blue her eyes are, like yours, and her long blond hair. Is she going to be OK? Now I feel bad."

"Honestly, it's fine. I should be allowed to go to Robotics Club, for crying out loud. It's like I can't have my own life or something."

Why am I rambling on about my dad? Gini makes me feel like I can be myself; like I can tell her everything. I can't believe other guys haven't noticed her. Sal and half the guys in my class have the hots for two of Gini's besties, Morgan and Sophie. They're at the top of the middle school social hierarchy. I have no idea who Lamar is hot for. In any case, Gini makes all her friends look basic. At least, that's how I see it.

* * *

ROBOTICS CLUB IS INTERESTING. I can't say it's something I'll be super passionate about, but it is fun being with Gini, and I like the other two kids on our team. They are both totally geeked out about robots.

I can't help but stew about my dad's text, though, and I dread going home. I'm not worried about what my dad is going to say to me. I'm scared about what I might say to him.

11
BUTTERFLY ILLUSION

I ride my bike slowly, splashing through puddles in the road. It rained all day but now the sun is out. I look for a rainbow and can't find one anywhere. *Bad omen*, I think. I remember the time my grandma told me the story of Noah and the Ark and how a rainbow is God's promise to never flood the earth again. My grandma believed that story 100%. I think I'm more like my dad in that I'm a bit of a skeptic, though I don't believe everything is a coincidence. Not anymore, anyway. And the reason for that is very simple and kind of ironic.

Lamar and I have spent a lot of time at the Natural History Museum. It was one of the only places our parents would drop us off and, if we stayed there and stayed together, we could go alone. Lamar has always been into drawing. He brings a notebook everywhere and takes private animation lessons.

One day a few years ago, we were standing in front of this new butterfly exhibit. It was a rainbow of butterflies. Literally, someone had made the display look like a rainbow starting with the tiniest ocean-blue butterfly at the bottom left and fanning the butterflies out across the case to the very biggest of the species. I never realized there were so many different types of butterflies. Some were as large as my hand. Some were shiny, like metal. Others were polka-dotted and striped.

I was in a bit of a trance, looking back and forth between the display and Lamar's drawing pad. I like to watch him draw. There's a magic to taking a blank page and creating something out of nothing, I think. Suddenly, Lamar looked up at me, his eyes big.

"If you look really close up," he said. "It looks like the butterfly wings are made of fur."

I walked up as close as I could get. "Whoa!" I exclaimed. "You're right. I never knew that before."

"And look at that one in the corner, doesn't it look like that butterfly has the same exact fur as a leopard?" He pointed. "And that one, it looks like zebra fur."

"That's really crazy!" I said. "How do you think that happened, like over time or what?"

"I don't know," Lamar said. "It's like some artist used those particular patterns and decided to put them on a couple of different species. If you think about it, flowers have some of the same patterns on them. That's crazy cool!"

"It's amazing." I replied.

"I didn't even know some of these colors existed. I mean, look at that mix of colors on that wing. I don't think I've ever even seen that color at the art store."

Sometimes, Lamar could be hard to follow. He has a bigger imagination than me. I've always known that, and I'm totally cool with it. It makes me proud he'd want to be my friend.

"It's like some great artist made these butterflies," he continued. "I mean, all of these patterns you see on other animals and stuff." He was staring at me, but I could see he was in his weird mind space where his brain is in overdrive.

"I don't know what you're talking about," I admitted.

He shook his head like he had a bit of a shiver. "Whoa," he says. "I literally right then had a full-on vision for my next animation. Picture this: some God-like being is standing in the middle of a field. He has an easel and starts painting these delicate butterfly wings. Each time He finishes one, puts His last stroke on the page, you start to see the wings and antennas wiggle. They wiggle ever so slightly, at first, and then come to life and fly off the page. God laughs and starts a new one. What do you think? Would that be a cool animation?"

I turned to look at the case again. "I like it," I say. "I want to see that one when you're done."

"Of course," he says, "I knew you'd get it. Help me pick what butterflies to include. What butterflies would you draw first, if you were God?"

That was Lamar at 11 years old. The dude is complex. I thank my lucky stars he picked me for a best friend, that's for sure.

* * *

I RIDE my bike straight into our garage, accidentally bumping into my sister's bike which crashes over into my dad's toolbox.

"Hey, you OK?" Dad yells through the kitchen window. I was hoping to sneak in and go straight to my room. Of course, I had to make a huge crashing noise like an idiot.

"I'm fine!" I yell.

I wonder if he's still mad about me not picking Jen up from school. I really hope he lets it go. I mean, if he says I need to take on more work, or whatever, I swear I'm going to lose it.

"Hey, bud," he says, the minute I head through the door. He's washing potatoes off in the sink. He looks up when the door closes and says, "Hey, bud," a second time. He has that look on his face where his forehead gets all wrinkly. He's upset.

"What's wrong?" I stand by the door. I bet he and Mom had a fight over Zoom.

"Oh nothing, kiddo, I'm fine."

"I can tell you're upset."

He nods to the counter stool, and I sit down.

"Just tell me, already," I say way grumpier than I mean to, but I'm sitting here having a mini panic attack and he's dragging things out.

"Some of my buddies were laid off today. Guys I've been working with for years, a couple of them."

"Who?"

Is this his way of telling me he's been laid off? That would be my family's luck lately. The luck of Balabrega.

"I don't think you'd know any of them. Some of these guys, they've been with GM for 30 years. How's a 50-something year old going to start over?" He looks at me, squinting an apologetic smile. "Sorry, bud. I shouldn't even be telling you this. I don't want you worrying about my work problems."

"Did you get laid off?"

Dad shook his head. "No, in fact, they asked me to take over for one of the supervisors. Essentially, I got a bump today, and a raise. I don't get how they make these decisions sometimes. We can really use that extra dough, but it sure puts me in a bad spot."

I don't know what to say. "I'm sorry." The tight feeling in my chest starts to fade a little. "You know what would cheer me up?" Dad asks.

"Ice cream?"

He laughs. "Yeah, that, too. No, I was thinking about the talent show, wanting to spunk things up a bit, you know?"

"Spunk? Is that even a word? It sounds gross."

He ignores me. "I bet we could modify a few of our tricks using laser lights. Kids love laser lights. We could even set something to music. You could pick the song. If we get it ready, we could even try it out at our show this weekend."

"What show? I didn't know we had a show."

Dad takes his glasses off and rubs his eyes. He is looking so much older than I ever remember. He yawns which makes me yawn. Suddenly, I feel tired, drained.

"I'm sorry. I must have forgotten to tell you," he says, like it's no big deal. "It was a last-minute booking. I've been pretty preoccupied with everything going on at work. It's a kid's birthday party. Two o'clock this Saturday."

"But I can't do it this weekend. I have a sleepover at Lamar's," I lie. Dad looks at me. I can tell he knows it's a sketchy story.

"Bud, why are you suddenly giving me so much grief over the shows?"

For a split second, I nearly tell him the truth, that I'm sick of doing what everyone else plans for me to do. But he's already had a bad day.

"Never mind," I end up saying. "What time's the show? Maybe I could get dropped off at Lamar's house after?" I'll have to text Lamar right away to tell him the plan.

"Sure, that's totally fine as long as you get your homework done before we head to the show. Deal?"

I nod and he puts his fist up for a fist bump.

"Cool beans!" he says. "Want to work on the new trick after dinner? You are gonna dig the lasers I bought."

"Actually, I'm kind of tired and I have a lot of homework. Can I go to my room until dinner?"

"Of course," he says. "No worries." He ruffles my hair. I try to pretend I'm not feeling angry. Heading to my room, I see I have a text from Gini. It's a song by Radiohead, one of my favorite bands. I put my headphones on and listen. Somehow, it totally matches my mood.

I know the last thing my dad needs right now is me being a total jerk. I'm not angry at him, really. My mom should be here, taking care of Jen and being there for my dad when he has a bad day. I'll never understand how she could leave us for two years. I don't even know why I'm thinking about it anymore.

I decide to go back down to the kitchen after an hour of

listening to different Radiohead songs. Dad is sitting next to Jen at the table, helping with her math homework. He looks up at me with his concerned look.

"Hey, I'm sorry I laid that on you earlier," he says.

"Laid what on him?" Jen pipes in.

"Nothing, kiddo." He looks at me. "Don't worry about me, Jayster. I'm good. Everything at work will be fine. It always works out."

I walk over and punch him in the arm. He grabs me and pulls me down onto his lap, tickling me like I'm a little kid. I have to admit, I sometimes like that he still does that. The day my mom left, I laid in my bed for a long time, feeling this horrible pit in my stomach, like I'd walked up to an open elevator shaft and fell in, and I kept falling and falling, trying to grab something to hold onto, to save myself.

When I feel close to my dad, like now, it's that loose cable I can grab and cling to. It's always fleeting, though. I wish that feeling, of being safe, would last longer but it always slips out of my grasp.

12
FAKE IT 'TIL YOU MAKE IT

I've been staying at Lamar's once a week, and he's been helping me get ready for the basketball tryouts. I know I'm pushing it with my dad, since this is my fourth weekend in a row staying over since school started. I really want to stay over at Lamar's both Friday and Saturday night, to see what he thinks about Gini. I need to talk to him about it and show him all the texts we've been sending to each other. I sweeten the deal, hoping to get my dad to agree.

"I'll get Jen home from school today," I say. "And I'll make her an afternoon snack."

Dad ruffles my hair a bit. "That'd be great, bud, thanks!"

"I can make my own snack!" Jen says, glaring at me.

"Whatever," I mumble. "So, um, Dad? Can I stay at Lamar's tonight?"

Dad stops making our lunches mid-peanut butter spread and stares at me for a minute. I keep my head down, shoveling Cap'n Crunch into my mouth, pretending like what I was asking was no big deal.

I started growing my hair out over the summer and my bangs are getting long enough to shade my eyes. Sometimes, I leave it like that, but most days I put loads of gel in it to pouf it up to one side. I have plans to meet Gini right after school and walk her to her bus. I'm thinking about trying to hold her hand.

I finally look up and Dad is back to making our sandwiches. "You want to stay over both nights? Fine, whatever, you can stay at Lamar's," he says, cutting the crust off the bread. I can tell he's discouraged and trying to hide it. "But I need you here after school. I'll come home a bit early so we can drill for an hour or two."

Maybe I shouldn't stay over at Lamar's both nights, I think. I imagine my dad's reaction to my saying I'd rather stay home, have a movie night or play games, practice our new tricks. I know that'd make him super happy, and I do want him to be happy.

I watch him, though my bangs, packing our lunches. I don't say anything. I take the last bite of my cereal and walk past my dad to put the bowl in the sink. Then, I rush off to my room to finish getting ready. I hear Jen whining about how if I get to stay at Lamar's, she wants to stay at her friend's house.

I hope my dad has already left for work, so we don't have to interact. I run down to grab my lunch and Jen to head out. He's there, still, sitting at the kitchen table drinking his coffee out of his *Best. Magician. Ever.* mug.

"Thanks, Dad," I say, putting my lunch in my backpack.

"So, you gonna be gone by the time I get home?"

"Um, yeah, probably. We want to get some b-ball in tonight." I still haven't told him about trying out for the basketball team yet, but I've been dropping little hints here and there.

"Don't forget we have that gig at 2 on Saturday. I think it might be a friend of that gal's family, Ragini. Is that her name? I think it was one of the kids at her brother's party. Parents called me Monday. Pretty last minute, but it's a gig."

"Yup, I remember, and I'll be home by 1 o'clock," I say. I'm surprised Gini hasn't said anything. Maybe she's not going to the party.

"Where's Jen? I don't want to be late again."

"JEN! Hurry it up, kiddo. Your brother is ready and waiting and he absolutely cannot be late!"

Jen comes in and wraps her arms around Dad's neck. He hugs her and looks at me.

"Get over here," he says, opening his arm wide. I go over and we hug.

***

DAD and I are in the basement practice area, running through our latest set of tricks with the new lasers and these color-changing hoops he bought from the Magic Bag. I have to admit, it's fun doing something new, but he keeps talking about how big it's going to go over at the talent show. I get so annoyed every time he brings it up. I try to change the subject.

"Dad, remember when we went through that phase of trying to trick Mom all the time?" I ask, laughing. He smiles and I keep at it, hoping he'll drop the whole talent show talk. "Like, the best one, I think, was when you taught me how to 'cut my finger off' with that fake blade. Remember that fake blood we got from Ray? It was so real looking. Mom literally screamed. So funny!"

"Remember the squeaking salt and pepper shakers?" he asks, laughing. "That's an oldie but goodie! I know you liked that fake blade trick. Do you want to tie something like that into the talent show act?"

UGH, he found a way to bring the talent show back up. Why can't we have a normal convo? What's that saying my grandpa likes – he's like a dog with a bone?

"Nah, I don't think so." I grab my Coke and take a swig, twirling the hoop on my arm.

"I know you're beat. Let's do the drill with the lasers one

more time and then we'll call it. I'll run through the lines. All right?"

"Did you type it out yet?" I ask. My dad writes all our scripts for us.

"I didn't have time. I'll run through it and type it out later. It's all up here." He taps his head and smiles.

"Dad, can we wait to run through it after I've seen the lines? I'm starting to get a headache and the guys needed me over by 7 p.m. so we can start our horror movie marathon."

I watch Dad's smile fade and his eyebrows furrow. Without saying anything, he sets the lasers down, gives me the OK sign and starts walking up the stairs.

"Dad?" I call to him.

He turns and gives me a half smile. "I'm just tired, bud. I didn't mean to walk away like that. I don't know what's coming over me lately. I'm sorry I've been so moody." He turns and starts back up the stairs, leaving all our equipment out. Normally, he likes to straighten up for the night. It's weird for him to walk away like that and leave it all out. Quickly, I put away the props we'd been using and head up.

After I pack my overnight bag, I find Dad and Jen sitting on the couch watching Pixar animated shorts. Dad looks up and asks, "You leaving?"

I nod. "What time are you going to pick me up tomorrow?"

"Be ready by noon, ok?"

"Sure, dad. Love ya."

"Love you, too. Have a good time, bud."

* * *

ANTHONY WANTS to stay over at Lamar's, too. Since getting Jen to take over as Dad's assistant was a no-go, Anthony says he wants to work on a foolproof plan to get me out of doing the talent show. I can use any help I can get, so I'm game. The only problem with Anthony lately is that awful cologne he's been wearing. I think he's hoping to attract Lydia by his "manly scent" as he calls it. Sal laughed so hard when he told us that, I thought he was going to pee his pants. We tease Anthony about it all the time and he does not care. It is strong stuff, though.

I told Gini about it when we met at her locker after school.

"It makes me sneeze," I said.

"OMG, that is too funny!" she said, laughing while she yanked her purple polka-dotted lunch bag from her locker before slamming it shut.

"I can't believe he likes Lydia. I wonder if she'll like him back. I can't see them together, at all."

"You have to promise not to tell anyone," I whispered, leaning in close. "He would totally kill me."

She held up two fingers and said, "Scouts honor."

I took my moment, right then, and reached out for her hand. She looked a tiny bit surprised, but then we laced our fingers together and I swear I could hear my own heart racing. Claire and I had held hands and it felt nice, but this was a different feeling all together. The minute Gini and I started holding hands, my fingers felt tingly, sort of like they'd fallen asleep. All I know is, I didn't want to stop holding her hand.

I can't remember a thing we talked about while we walked. Before I knew it, we were standing in front of her bus, and I could feel eyes on the back of my head. She gave me a quick hug before leaping up the bus steps. I turned around to peer through the windows and saw Gini's two besties grinning right at me. Sophie gave me a thumbs up.

Gini leaned over her to wave, and they all giggled and started talking at once. I could feel my cheeks burning. That is one bad thing about being so pale skinned. My cheeks are always turning red.

* * *

MIDDLE SCHOOL IS NO PLACE FOR MAGIC

I FEEL SUPER-CHARGED PEDALING fast up the road. It's Friday, Gini and I held hands, I don't have any homework, and, besides the one show, the weekend is FREE!

The air is starting to feel slightly crisp. I can smell a bonfire going. Leaves crunch under my tires. The trees are at their peak color. At least, that's what our science teacher was saying. Riding closer to Langdon Avenue, I hear drums echoing from UM's band practice field. I'm sure they're gearing up for the big football game against Ohio State. My parents are not all that into Michigan football, but Lamar's and Anthony's families watch every game together, usually at Lamar's house. Tailgate food is the best.

I look down at my hands gripping the handlebars and they still feel slightly tingly. Maybe this fall won't be so bad after all.

13
PUFF THE MAGIC DRAGON

It only takes eight minutes by bike to get to Seventh Street Park from my house. Lamar is already there, shooting hoops. We practice for a good three hours – well past dark. We play under the city lights. Most nights, there are a few homeless people hanging out in the park because the shelter is only two blocks up the street. A couple of the guys join us for a game of two on two. They tower over us and, of course, they crush it. We've gotten to know one of them, Bob, and he always tells us the same story, about the time he was playing ball for Pioneer High School, how he made the winning three-pointer.

When Bob and his friend leaves, I tell Lamar all about Gini – even the parts about holding hands and the hug by the bus and the secret plan I'm hatching to take her on a date downtown for her birthday. Her birthday is in two weeks, October 16th.

We talk through how I should ask her. I'm going to do it Monday. My armpits sweat thinking about it. Lamar thinks I should bring a balloon to school with a note inside that she'd have to pop to get out.

"Nah, too elaborate," I say. "I don't want to make it a spectacle. I was thinking I could work it into one of my easier magic card tricks. Gini's been asking me to show her some of my 'magic moves.' That's what she calls it. I really like that she doesn't think magic is goofy."

"It's not goofy, dude," Lamar says. "I think she'll like that."

"You do?"

"Yes, that sounds sweet," he says. "Let's get going. Mom's making the wings tonight because the tailgate's starting early. She said we could have some when we get home."

"Awesome, let's go!" I grab my bike and we start walking through the park, back up toward his block.

"What do you think of Gini?" I ask Lamar. It's a little awkward on the sidewalk with me walking my bike, so I motion for us to walk on the street. "I mean, it's crazy I never even noticed her before. Now, it's like I can't stop thinking about her!"

Is this what it feels like to be in love? I wonder. *Like levitating?*

"She's really nice," he says, shrugging. I notice Lamar is being more serious than usual. He was kind of in his head the whole time we were playing, come to think of it.

Lamar took a deep, long breath. That usually means he has something to tell me. I hope it isn't something bad about Gini.

"I'm happy for you, dude. I mean, it's crazy how quick you're catching feels for each other. All those years we went to school together and you two barely talked. Now you're a couple and everything. Are you're, like, planning to kiss her?"

I blush, which makes me feel stupid. I hope he doesn't notice.

"Sure. I mean, yes, at some point."

He dribbles the ball a couple of times and smiles, slyly. "You know that date you're planning might be a good time."

"I was kinda thinking that, too." I give him a light punch on the arm, and we laugh.

"So, what about you? Do you like anyone? Or..." I have a strange feeling that's what his sighs are about. Is he jealous of me and Gini? Maybe he thinks she'll take up all my time and we won't be able to hang as much. OR maybe he likes someone, and it hasn't worked out.

There's a long pause and we keep walking, me with my bike, Lamar with his basketball. Lamar dribbles the ball a few times. Then, he says, "Dude, I'm gay." He takes a big breath again.

I feel like the breath's been knocked out of me.

"What?" I stop dead in my tracks and look at him. "What do you mean? How do you know? Are you sure?"

Lamar catches the basketball which was slipping from his hands. He laughs, which surprises me. "Um, yeah, I'm pretty sure. I'm surprised you never guessed, actually."

"Um. Um..."

That's how you respond? What the hell?! I scold myself. BUT I legit don't know what to say. My brain is whirring with all these memories of me and Lamar. I've known him since we were three. I suddenly feel stupid. It makes sense. When I think about it for a minute, it feels right. I mean, I've NEVER heard Lamar mention a girl that way, or anyone, really.

"And, in case you're wondering," he added. "I'm not at all attracted to you."

"I hope not!" OMG, I didn't mean to say that. Lamar laughs hard, which makes me smile.

It's not a big deal, I tell myself. Then, I think about school. When Lamar comes out at school, I'm sure he'll be picked on, maybe even by the other basketball players.

"Dude, you're like a brother to me," Lamar says. It hits me that he must think I'm upset about him saying he's not attracted to me. *Oh God,* I think, *now he's explaining why he's not into me and that's not it at all.* "We've known each other since we were, like, three," Lamar says. "It would be really gross. Plus, you're straight. I'm not attracted to straight guys. I like other gay guys."

We're nearly to the big United Methodist Church on Miller. I'm feeling lightheaded and out of breath, like the way I felt at Gini's. *Are panic attacks going to be a regular thing for me now?* I can feel tears starting to well up and I get this stupid lump in my throat. I don't want to cry. I REALLY don't want to cry. I don't even know why I feel like crying in the first place.

"Can we stop a minute?" I ask, walking over the front steps of the church. I sit down and put my head in my hands. It's everything – my mom, the stupid talent show, the basketball tryouts coming up. And now there's this thing with Lamar.

Why does everything have to change, I think. *I need things with Lamar to stay like they were and always have been.* I feel bad, like, super selfish. I know it's not all about me but that's what I'm thinking, to be honest.

"You OK?" Lamar asks gently. He sits beside me. I can feel he's waiting for me to say something and there's this odd tension between us.

"I need a minute. Can we sit for a minute?"

"Sure, that's fair," he says. Then, Lamar gets up and starts pacing in front of the steps, dribbling the ball. I look up at him, at the concerned look on his face, and it hits me hard how much it must have taken for him to do this, to tell me he's gay. If Lamar is really going to come out, like at school and everything, he's the one who is going to have to face a ton of change. He could lose friends. He might be bullied. His own family, even, might not accept him for who he is. I've always felt like the one who needs his help. This is the first time in our lives Lamar has ever needed me. Suddenly, I feel a little steadier. It no longer feels like the ground is moving underneath my feet.

"Do your parents know?" I ask.

He stops pacing and, to my relief, even kind of smiles. "Yes, when I told them, my mom said she suspected I was. My dad was surprised, but he seems OK now. I figured you knew. I guess you didn't. I'm sorry–."

"What? No, it's fine," I interrupt. "It's not that."

He nods, but still looks unsure.

"It did surprise me, but I mean, I totally get it. I'm sorry-"

"For what?"

"For being so distracted with my own stuff. I'm sure it wasn't easy, you know..."

We stare at each other for a few seconds.

"I'm sorry you didn't feel like you could tell me sooner."

"We're good," he says, smiling, and the tension is gone. Lamar starts walking and I get up from the church steps, pick up my bike and walk a little bit behind him so we can stay on the sidewalk.

"Well, don't you have any other questions you want to ask me?" he says, moving to the road and waiting for me. "You're always full of questions. Come on! I know you're dying to ask me stuff."

"What about Lydia? How did she react?"

"She's been nicer to me," Lamar says. "A LOT nicer, actually. You know my sister better than any of my friends do. She'll never come out and tell me exactly what she's thinking but I can guess. I bet she thinks we can gossip about boys together, go shopping together, you know? She's been chill, though. Still her same weird self, and I'm still myself."

We both laugh. "I'm sorry, but I can't see you doing that. At least, not the shopping part. You're a jock. I mean, you're one of the best basketball players in our whole class."

"Yup, I'm kind of an artsy jock," he says.

We walk for about a block without saying anything. I still feel a little bit stupid. I mean, if I'm oblivious about something as huge as this about my best friend, and clueless about my own mom's life, what else have I been completely not seeing?

"How long have *you* known?" I ask.

He doesn't pause, not even for a second. "Since the end of sixth grade."

"That long? Why didn't you tell me?" I can't help the hurt that came out in my voice.

He sighs and looks down. "Look, it's not because I don't trust you. I had to be ok with it first. Like, you can't tell anybody this – not even Sal and especially not Anthony – but I had a huge crush on Mr. Drury. It was bad. I couldn't even talk when he was around and it kind of scared me."

"Mr. Drury? Are you joking?" I start to snicker a little.

"Yes," he interrupts. "And don't laugh. Big jerk! You had a crush on Ms. Rose. I'm sorry, but Mr. Drury is A LOT better looking than her, and he smells better, too."

I laugh again. "OK, OK, you're right!"

"Anyway, back then I didn't know if it was, like, a bi thing. I thought, you know, maybe that's what was going on because before Mr. Dray, I didn't crush on anybody. But then, at camp this summer..."

"What? Did something happen? Was it at Blue Lake?"

"Yup, it was at art camp in June." He pauses again.

"Well, what happened? Come on, you have to tell me now!"

Lamar looks at me. "So...I met someone. His name is Melvin. He's from the west side of the state. We kissed before we left, and we've been texting every day since. Then, right before school started, he suddenly stopped texting. I've called him, like, ten times. It really hurts. That's how I know, for sure, that I'm gay. I told my parents because they kept asking me if I was OK, and I knew they were really worried about me. I didn't want to say anything to you because you were going through so much with your mom and all, but you seem better now."

Four weeks. Months, if you count when he first met Melvin. He's been going through all of that alone. I feel like the worst friend. I'm so into my own stupid problems that I don't even notice what Lamar's going through. I walk up and put my arm around his shoulder.

"You want me to kick Melvin's butt, or what? How dare he ghost you!"

Lamar laughs. "No, it's fine. I'll get over it. I'm starting to get over it."

"Screw that dude!" I say, dropping my arm so I can park my bike next to his garage. We start heading up to his house.

"Anything else you want to ask me?" he asks.

"Um, so," I say, "do you like anyone new?"

"Not the way I like Melvin, but I have my little crushes. Nothing serious, though."

"OK. One last thing, though. Don't hide that kind of stuff from me, k? Like, if you ever do have a serious crush, will you tell me?"

"Of course, dude. From now on, I'm not going to keep things like that from my best friend." I nod.

He grins and I look away for a second. Again, I could feel myself tearing up. *Ugh*, I think, *just great*. I know he hates mushy stuff, but I stop for a minute and put my hand on his arm. I tell him, "Lamar, you're my best friend. No matter what."

I see tears spring up in his eyes, too. He nods.

"I feel like we should hug or something," I say.

Lamar laughs. Then we both started laughing. He puts his hand out, pointing at me. I point back and we do our handshake and little bro hug at the end. I still have a small, nagging worry that this will somehow change things, but I push it aside. I'm getting better at that – at not thinking about things that bother me.

14
PLAN B, C & D

JAY'S "FOOL-PROOF" PLAN TO GET OUT OF THE TALENT SHOW

1. Fake an illness the morning of. (More difficult than it sounds.)
2. Pull the fire alarm right as you take the stage. (Anthony to do the dirty deed; Sal and Lamar will be the lookouts.)
3. Orchestrate a minor skateboarding accident and play up injury.
4. Dye hair the night before, pretend to get dye in eyes leading to temporary (fake) blindness.
5. Sacrifice one tip of one finger the night before. Details TBA.
6. Tell your dad the truth. Probably your best bet.

– Anthony D. Fuller

15
ABRACADABRA

Dad ended up being OK with me staying in Robotics Club, as long as I don't slack off with my homework or with our practices, which we have a couple nights a week. Dad is laid back about most stuff, except when it comes to getting our tricks down right. He never seems to get tired of practicing. I'm bored stiff with the whole routine, except for the new laser trick.

I don't mean to, but I end up complaining to Gini about it while we walk together to Robotics Club.

"I understand," she says, "you can't tell your dad you are tired of doing the shows because you feel guilty and are worried it will disappoint him, right?"

I nod. It's a relief to hear her say she gets it.

"The main problem is that my dad is under a lot of pressure with other things right now, and he would have to come up with a whole new routine. My mom's gone. I mean, not gone forever, I don't think. You know what I mean. Plus, he got this new promotion with a lot more responsibility."

"It must be hard for you, though, working with your dad all

the time. You work a lot, and, I mean, we're just kids. You're only thirteen."

It is hard, I think. *Not many kids are, like, their parent's show business partner.*

"I know it's weird-"

"No, it's not that. Not weird, just hard."

"Yeah, my dad has a lot going on with my mom going to back to school," I keep blabbing. "She used to work at Second Story Books and now, even though he got a raise not too long ago, things are still pretty tight." I can feel my face flush. Three of our houses could fit into Gini's huge place so they clearly don't have money issues.

"You're too young to have to worry about your parents' finances and stuff," she says, surprising me. "I wish your dad wouldn't put that on you."

She intertwines her fingers with mine. She has thin, soft fingers. We're standing close to each other, near the locker room door. I mean, we are WELL within kissing range. I feel goofy, happy and nervous all of a sudden, all at the same time. Gini's looking at me, staring right into my eyes. It's almost like she *wants* me to kiss her. I can feel my hands getting sweaty and wonder if she's getting grossed out by it. She doesn't seem to notice. My heart feels fluttery. I've never felt fluttery before, like, in my entire life. I don't know what to do, so I keep talking.

"So, that's how we've always been, me and my dad. He tells me stuff I guess a lot of dads wouldn't. In some ways, I like it. We're more like best friends."

"Well, that part is nice," she says. "I definitely wouldn't say my parents are friends."

Her voice has changed. It sounds soft and dreamy. She is stroking my hand with her thumb. *Is this her way of flirting with me? Does she want me to kiss her?* The heart flutters are turning into thumps. I wonder if anyone wonders where we are. We're at least five minutes late to club. I'm certainly not going to say anything!

Gini scoots even closer to me and whispers, "I wish I had that with my parents, actually. Do you think he's like that because you started doing the magic shows with him? How old were you, anyway?"

"I was eight when he let me join the show. And five when I did my first magic trick."

"What was it, your first trick?"

"It was a cup and ball trick, where you put a ping pong ball under one of three cups, mix them up and make someone guess where it went." *Is my breath bad? Why didn't I take that gum from Lamar when he offered it?*

"Neat! You learned that when you were five?"

"Yeah, it's pretty simple."

"Will you show me how to do it someday?"

I grin. "I don't think I can do that. A magician never reveals his tricks," I tease, laughing at the scowl forming on her face. I can't believe it, but now I'm sounding flirty, and it's working.

"Jay! Are you being serious?" She pokes me in the ribs, lightly.

"Oh, I'm deadly serious." I half-smile.

She sticks her lower lip out in a pout, which makes me melt.

"I'm teasing, I'm teasing," I relent. "Of course, I'll show you."

She starts tickling me in the ribs. I'm giggling and playing along, but what I feel like doing is kissing her right on the lips.

"Stop, I give. Uncle." I back into a locker, my hands raised. She stares at me, grinning. The way she looks at me makes me blush.

"I win," she says, shyly now.

"Actually, I do have a trick for you."

I pull out the cards I'd prepped to ask her on our downtown date. *Why are my hands shaking? I can't look at her and focus.* For a minute, the whole trick flies out of my head. I stare down the hallway to make sure no one is watching us and take a few deep breaths.

"OK, you wanna see?" I ask, finally able to look at her again.

"Yes, of course!" I can see her eyes shining, so I lay it on thick. Lamar helped me come up with the whole thing.

"So, to tell you the truth, I made this trick up special for you," I tell her.

"Really?! That's so sweet." Gini claps her hands a few times. I hope she's not disappointed. I've really built it up now.

First, I do a simple overhand shuffle and then I do the slightly more impressive Hindu shuffle. (I know, ironic since Gini is Hindu!) I weave the cards the way I practiced, hold the cards out and ask her to pick one.

"Now, put it back in the pile anywhere you like."

I cut the cards and then locate my key card so I can have her pick from the top. She'll draw the card I've written on.

"Is that your card?" I ask.

"No, there's writing on this one."

"What does it say?"

She reads it aloud. "Will you go out with me for your birthday?" Gini looks up, her eyes wide. She starts to nod her head.

"Wait! Before you answer that, is this your card?" I pull out the one I've tracked – a Queen of Hearts. Gini gasps and takes the card from my hands. "How?"

I laugh. "Well, will you go?"

Gini holds both cards to her chest. Then she hugs me, right there in the hallway. I'm so glad the only person who sees is Daryn. He's one of the nicer janitors who I helped when I was forced to clean up the schoolyard at the beginning of the year. He winks at me as he walks by.

Gini hears him behind her and quickly pulls away.

"So, um, what are you doing for your birthday? It's this coming Saturday, right? Do you have any plans Friday?"

"No, not that I know of. Not on Friday."

OK, it's going good so far.

"You know how I told you about some of the cool places I wanted to show you downtown?"

Gini looks a little stunned when I say that, which scares me.

"Downtown? I don't think my parents will let me go with you, like, unchaperoned. They told me I can't date until I'm 16, two years from now. I know it's a bummer."

I take a deep breath. *Keep going – say what you practiced,* I tell myself.

"Well, I wouldn't want to get you in any kind of trouble with your parents. But there is a way we could go downtown together, and they'd never find out."

"How?"

At least she is willing to listen to the plan. I hold my hand out to her and we start walking down the hall again, toward the science lab where they hold Robotics Club. "See, I'm thinking you could tell them that you're meeting friends at the downtown library. Maybe your friends would even go there with you. We could all take the city bus down. The bus station is right across from the main library. Do you think your friends would cover for you? I mean, it would only be two hours. We won't go far from the library. Technically, we are friends, so it's not exactly a lie. We could go to Starbucks and then down to the practice field to listen to the marching band. And maybe go to Graffiti Alley. Have you ever been there?"

She was shaking her head no. I knew she was right. She might get in trouble if she was caught sneaking around with me.

"I know!" she exclaims, "Why don't you come to the downtown library, and we can stay there together? That way, if my parents show up or something, I'll be there, and we could say we bumped into each other. Maybe we could get some of your friends to go, too?"

I inadvertently bite my bottom lip. Her brows furrowed.

"I'm sorry," she says.

"You don't have to be sorry," I tell her. Now I feel weird for even asking her to do something like that. I feel like I need to explain how I came up with the screwy plan in the first place.

"It's that... so... remember at your brother's party when you said you feel different from the people in your neighborhood? And you also said your family really doesn't get downtown a whole lot. I mean, you've lived so close to downtown all your life and never really seen it the way I do. When I go downtown, I can walk around for hours and not see a soul I know. I like that, you know, the feeling of being invisible and with people at the same time."

Gini was nodding, but I really couldn't tell if I was making sense to her or not.

"And there's, like, so many different types of people. It's weird NOT to be different, you know? You can dress any way you want in Ann Arbor. Nobody cares what you look like and stuff like that."

"Really?" She was smiling.

"I'm not saying this to try to talk you into going. I only want you to know, like, that I thought you'd like the places I like. I thought it might make you feel the same way, kinda free. And you should feel that way. You're a beautiful person, inside and out."

UGH, stop rambling.

Gini stands there, her hands hanging by her sides, staring at me. I do know mushy eyes when I see them. It's the same look my mom used to give me when I'd run up to her totally randomly and give her a hug or tell her I love her, and that thought gives me a slight pang in my chest. I push my mom out of my brain.

"Gini?" I say. Looking at me that way, she's making my palms all sweaty again. Suddenly, she moves closer and put her hand on my shoulder.

"OK," she says.

"OK?"

"Yes, I want to do that with you, Jay. I'll ask Morgan and Soph if they'll cover for me. That's a good idea."

"But Gini, I don't know." Now I'm having doubts. "I mean, if we get caught, how much trouble would you be in, exactly?"

"They would probably give me the silent treatment. That's what happened to my cousin when she got caught sneaking out of her bedroom window to go make out with her boyfriend. My whole family was not allowed to speak to her for a month. And I'd be grounded."

"That sounds awful!" I exclaim.

Gini shrugs. "I mean, my parents are ridiculously strict. I always do everything they want me to. Look at what some of the kids in our grade are doing, already. I'm a saint, compared, and I'm kinda sick of it. Besides, hopefully, they'll never know," she says, and walks into the Robotics Club lab.

16

MAGIC CEMETERIES AND PIZZERIAS

"Do you remember the first time you performed a magic trick in front of other people?" Gini asks. We're sitting in the courtyard, eating lunch together. It's kind of chilly and she is sitting close, leaning into me. I look around and see some kids glancing our way, probably wondering what she's doing with me – geek-a-zoid of the year. I instantly feel proud and put my arm around her waist. She scoots in closer.

"Yeah, I remember exactly what it was, actually." I speak.

There was one trick in particular that drew me into magic. It was this trick where my dad made a box of crayons disappear. I'd already learned a few simple card tricks by the time I started working on it. The crayon trick was a challenge. When I asked my dad to show me the crayon trick, he said very seriously, "Are you sure you want to know? Because once you start learning some of these secrets, you'll be obsessed with figuring all the tricks out. Then, some of the magic will be gone for you. That's how it was for me when I was first started out."

After I thought about it for a minute, I was like, *I have to know how it's done. I have to figure it out.* So, he sat me on his lap with this box of crayons from the show. Here, he says, open it.

I notice Gini is looking at me, waiting for my answer. "The first trick I ever performed with my dad was this one where it looks like you can make crayons in an eight-count box disappear," I tell her.

"How does it work?" she asks.

"You take this normal box of crayons and cut each crayon in half. Then you glue them all together and then glue a couple of toothpicks on each side. You use the toothpicks to hold them in place, so they look totally new and lined up in that little crayon window. Then, you let them fall beneath the window, using the toothpicks to move them down, and – poof – they're gone."

"It sounds kind of crafty, making the tricks."

"Oh, yeah, it is. We spend at least part of the week crafting for the show. That's always been a big part of it. We try to make the props ourselves because it can get expensive. Sometimes, though, you have to hire people. There's a place about an hour and a half from here called Colon where they can make all sorts of sets and tricks. Colon is known as the Magic Capitol of the World."

"What? Really? How come I've never heard of it?" She looked at me sideways.

"I'm not making that up. It's this tiny town and they have, like, three magic shops. They hire metal workers and wood workers and artists, and they ship their props to magicians all over the world. My dad is friends with the owner of one of the shops, Ray. He has so much, like, old magician stuff. I'm talking props from super-famous magicians. Ray is a ventriloquist, so he collects all these old dolls that magicians have used over the years."

"Wait a minute. You know an actual ventriloquist?"

"Yeah, I know a few."

"Wow, that is really cool! I've never even been to a magic shop."

"Seriously?! I can't believe that. We have to take you there sometime. I'll ask my dad about it tonight. The whole town is all about magic. The school team is the Magis, and they have this pizza joint with all of these photos of famous magicians who have been to the town. There's even a secret door they made from a bookcase that leads to a big pizza party room. I always wanted to have a pizza party there, but Dad says it's too far. They have a ton of magicians buried in the town cemetery. These famous magicians are buried there - Harry Blackstone and Percy Abbott and a bunch more."

I look over and Gini is grinning at me like crazy.

"I probably sound like a total geek right now," I say.

Gini leans her head on my shoulder for a minute. I love it when she does that. A group of girls across the courtyard start whispering. I lean my head onto hers and take her hand.

"Sorry I kinda went off for a sec."

Gini lifts her head and looks at me.

"Jay, I think it's really cool that you know all of this stuff. Most guys only want to talk about sports, cars, video games, and stuff like that. At least, it seems like that's what they talk about. I really want to go to that town with you someday and see it. It sounds super fun!"

"Really?"

"Well, yeah, especially if they have a cool pizza place with a secret room. Who wouldn't want to see that?!"

I could see she meant it. Her eyes seemed to sparkle when she looked at me. It made my heart race fast and I wanted to kiss her so badly, right there in the courtyard. It felt like I was literally walking on a cloud the rest of the day.

* * *

I TOOK the long route home from school, cutting through Miller Park. Talking to Gini made me think about when I was first learning to do magic. From the day I learned the crayon trick on, I didn't really *watch* the shows anymore, I *studied* them.

It's one thing to know how to do the steps in a trick but you also have to perform. My dad has these distraction techniques. He's especially good at using comedy to distract the audience. It's like you stack these things on top of each other to do magic. You learn the tricks, then you learn the distraction technique, then you learn the act. You put it all together for the show. It takes years of practice to even do a full 30-minute set straight through and be good at it.

When I became obsessed with magic, my dad was thrilled. He'd stop whatever he was doing if I asked him to show me the steps of a trick. He'd do the whole trick all the way through, in slow motion, and then he'd break it down for me. First, he'd do step one and two and then I'd try to copy him. I was sloppy at first. It takes a lot of hand and eye coordination, which I didn't have a lot of when I was five, six, seven years old. But Dad never lost his patience with me. Mom always says, "One thing I love about your dad is that he has the patience of Job."

We'd drill. Dad would tell me to do it again and again. Sometimes, he'd have to show me a second time. He'd nod to have me do it a third time. Then, we'd move on to the next part and so on until I could do the entire trick all the way through. Then, we'd drill the entire trick over and over.

I guess it's how you get good at anything. You aren't gonna hit a nail on the head the first time you try or play Bach the first time you sit at a piano. Like with playing the tuba or getting good at basketball – if you want to be good at something, you practice.

I think the thing that drove me to keep practicing was getting to be with my dad. We spent a lot of time together. And I could tell he loved it as much as I did. That was probably the best part. He'd get so excited to show me a new trick or something he'd modified from a one-person act to a two-person, so I could be in the show. After we drilled until the trick was perfect, that was an awesome feeling. He'd whoop and clap. "YES, that's my boy!" It was like we had our own special club.

The past year or so, though, it all started feeling old. I want to have a couple weeks off here and there or even a couple of months to be a kid and not focus on shows. School is getting harder, too. Algebra is already kicking my butt and it's only October. Plus, I want to try new things or, some days, do NOTHING. It seems like I never get a break.

This past year, Dad's moods started being very up and down. I could tell something was off with Mom and Dad. They seemed distant, both from each other and us. He yelled at me a couple of times for forgetting steps or not learning a new part as quickly as he thought I should. The practicing and shows that used to be fun feel like nothing but work lately. I don't know.

I used to think I would be a magician like my dad when I grew up, even if only as a hobby. But now I don't know. I really don't know anymore.

17

A MAGIC MELODY

Ragini means a melody; music; love. I always think it's cool when the meaning of someone's name kind of matches who they are.

My real name is James David after both my dad and Mom's dad. James means "supplanter," or basically someone who follows. When I found that out, I was like, *what the heck?* I mean, that doesn't fit me at all. I don't feel like either a James or a Jimmy, which is what my dad goes by. I'm glad my parents started calling me Jay when I was a baby and it stuck. Jay means "to rejoice," which also doesn't exactly fit me, but it's WAY better than "supplanter."

When I looked up what Ragini means in Hindi, I knew I had to do something with it for her birthday. Grandpa Dave, my mom's dad, was an electrician for the University of Michigan before he retired. He also does a lot of woodworking and even has an Etsy store. I hit him up to help me make something for Gini, and he was totally cool with it.

Grandpa used to come to our house at least once a week for dinner, but I haven't seen him in nearly three weeks. I asked Dad about it, and he told me and Jen that Grandpa has been having some problems with his diabetes. Now I feel bad. With school and everything else going on, I haven't been over to my grandpa's in a long time. I'm a little upset that my dad didn't tell us about his diabetes acting up earlier.

* * *

ON TUESDAY, after I dropped Jen off and made her a snack, I rode my bike to my grandpa's house. It's a solid ten blocks, mostly downhill all the way there. You might think Michigan is a flat state. We do have a lot of flat farms and woods, but Ann Arbor is hilly. You don't notice it much when you're walking or driving but when you bike, you really feel it.

Grandpa lives in a neighborhood called the Old West Side, near the city YMCA. That's where my mom grew up. To get there, I usually stick to side streets, biking down through Seventh Street Park, over to Huron Avenue and past the Y. There is one big hill that I have to pedal up on the way there, in the last block to his house. It's pretty steep. Sometimes, if it's crowded with cars, I'll get off and walk my bike up.

Their house is over 100 years old. It's not super fancy, like some of the houses on the Old West Side, but it is a decent size. It has a glassed-in front porch. That's my favorite room in their house. The wall near their front door is lined with shelves. Grandma kept toys, books and craft stuff out there. On the far end is a comfy light blue couch. On the table near the couch is a framed photo of Martin Luther King, Jr. and one of his quotes: "An individual has not started living until he can rise above the narrow confines of his individualistic concerns to the broader concerns of all humanity."

My grandma and grandpa met at a Martin Luther King, Jr. speech in 1962, when he came to Hill Auditorium. They were both 16. It was standing room only and my grandpa gave up his seat so my grandma could sit down. I always thought that was a cool story. How amazing would that be, to see Martin Luther King, Jr. speak, and meet the love of your life all in one day? *Best love story ever*, I think.

Before my grandma died, she was a counselor for people who were trying to stop drinking and doing drugs. She had more than three hundred people at her funeral, so many I didn't even know, and people were sobbing. It was surprising. "All walks of life," my grandpa said when he walked up to me at the wake. I could tell it made him really proud. Some of the people she helped stood up at her funeral and talked about how she had saved their lives. Grandpa started crying during that part and he couldn't stop, not even when he got up to speak. I felt like I might lose it, seeing him like that, so I focused on Jen who was also crying by that point. I put my arm around her shoulder and kept whispering that it was going to be all right.

Before that, I didn't even know women could have massive heart attacks and be gone so fast. After Grandma died, I was scared everything would change. I didn't even know if Grandpa would stay in their house without her. But Grandpa pretty much left things where they belonged. My grandma's China dishes were still there, in the China cabinet, along with her little bell collection with the names of all the states they'd gone to. Grandma liked things with mushrooms on them, like mushroom-shaped salt and pepper shakers and this tiny elf family with mushroom caps for hats. I always touched the smooth, glass top of the artsy orange mushroom that sat on the entry table.

Even though Grandma died two years ago, and the house still feels the same, I miss her a lot. Being at their house instantly makes me feel calmer, but also sad not to hear her voice call out to me when I walk in, not to smell her cooking or feel her hugs.

I always head straight to Grandma's writing desk to grab a

piece of candy from the top drawer. Grandpa has been refilling the candy stash for me and Jen the last couple of years.

I stand there a minute before calling out for my grandpa because something feels off. I can't put my finger on it. Everything looks the same.

Then, it hits me. It's not this house that has changed, but mine. I can feel myself getting angry at my mom, which makes me feel anxious again. I close my eyes and take a couple deep breaths, spreading my hands out in front of me. *I'm not going to let that BS ruin my time*, I say, repeating the mantra I'd come up with. I start feeling better, calmer.

When I open my eyes, Grandpa is standing in the kitchen doorway, staring at me with his bushy eyebrows, all furrowed. He looks worried, so I smile.

"Hi, Grandpa! Thanks for helping me with this," I say, walking in from the entryway and giving him a quick hug.

"Good to see ya, kiddo!" Grandpa says, squeezing my shoulder. I grab a Coke out of the fridge, and we head to the workshop in his garage. I notice he's using a cane and has a slight limp. I think about asking him about what's going on with that but decide not to. Grandpa isn't big on talking about his health. He doesn't like talking about his time in the Vietnam War, either. I learned that one day when I got curious and started badgering him with questions. Grandma gave me a look and shut that down quick.

When I'd called earlier in the week, I told him about Gini and what I wanted to make for her birthday. I tried to find a Hindu symbol for music and the closest one I could find was the symbol for Om, which wasn't the right fit. I Googled symbols for music, and I found this cool picture of a heart "wearing" headphones.

I think it will look neat engraved on a wood plaque. I want to carve Gini's name inside the heart. I texted the image to Grandpa to see what he thought. Grandpa texted back saying he was going to buy a new engraving drill and we could get something like this done lickety-split. He had the square wooden piece all sanded down for me.

"This is great, Grandpa," I say, picking it up, turning it over. "What kind of wood is this? It smells really good."

"Oak," he tells me. "Have to use a hard wood for this kind of stuff. It'll turn out pretty. Now, I can do some of the engraving and show you how it's done. Then, you can etch her name on there. How does that sound?"

He pulls what look like a dentist's drill out of a case and flicks it on. It even sounds like a dentist drill. Then he hands me some plastic-type paper and a pencil and tells me to trace the heart image onto it. I grab the copy I printed out from my backpack.

"Is this going to be used to trace it on or something?" I ask.

"Yup. So..." he grins, and I know what's coming. "About this gal, what's her name?" Grandpa loves to tease.

"Ragini, but pretty much everyone calls her Gini."

"Like genie in a bottle?"

I nod and pull a stool up to the workbench.

"She must be pretty special for you to want to make this for her. I dream of Jeannie with the light brown hair," Grandpa starts to sing while I start tracing the heart and headphone picture onto the template.

"Ragini means music, in Hindi."

"You don't say?" Grandpa replies. "That's interesting."

While I draw, he starts rooting around for something. The sawdust smells like the woods at Harrisville State Park, up north. It makes me think of the secret place I'd discovered with my cousin when we were camping there, a wooded spot near a small path to the rocky beach. Every year, we camp at Harrisville for a week with my mom's brother Todd, my Aunt Cassy (Uncle Todd's wife), my cousins and now my grandpa. They live in California, so we don't get to see them very much. My dad's an only kid, so there are no cousins on that side. It's always a blast being with my cousins, Simon and Noelle. Simon is a year and a half older than me.

You can see Lake Huron from our special spot in the campground. We like to go there and read comics, swim, watch the freighters and sailboats float by, off in the distance.

"Now, kiddo," Grandpa said. "Do you want Ragini to be able to set this on a nightstand or hang it up?"

"I don't know. What do you think?" I'm nearly done with the tracing. I show Grandpa and he nods.

"Perfect! Tell you what, let's make it so she can decide how she wants it displayed. After we're all done with the engraving and, I assume, you want to stain it, too, we'll nail on one of these sawtooth mounts, plus drill a hole at the bottom and she can put one of these little wooden pegs here, like so." He illustrates it so I can see what he's talking about.

"Sounds great to me," I say. This is going to turn out way nicer than I'd imagined. Grandpa coming through in a pinch, as usual.

Grandpa looks at me with his eyeglasses half hanging off his honker and a smallish smile forming on his lips. I know that means he's going to tease me about something or other.

"Now, back to the inquisition. About this Gini gal, how did you two meet?" He starts looking through his drill bits, rooting through his tool bench.

"We met in kindergarten, but we only started dating a couple of weeks ago after Dad and I did a show for her brother's birthday. She seems to like magic, which is good, I guess. She's also really into robotics."

"Dating, huh? Sounds official. Well, she sounds like a very nice girl," Grandpa winked at me. "And how is everything else going? You missing your mom?"

"I'm good," I lie. I don't want to upset Grandpa by telling him how angry I've been with her. I suspect my mom has already said something about my not wanting to talk with her.

"I'm more worried about Jen," I continue. "She's always Zooming with Mom. But, good news, Dad got a promotion. You heard about that, right?" I am getting good at changing the subject.

"Yes, I did and I'm real proud of your dad. I heard your mom's coming back from Iowa in a little over a month. She called me last night to let me know the exact date, November 25th, day before Thanksgiving."

"Yeah, for a long weekend." That makes me think, again, about the talent show. I've pretty much ruled out all of Anthony's hare-brained ideas, except the fire alarm. It might come down to that one.

"It'll be good to have your mom home for a few days; don't you think?"

When I don't say anything, he drops it. Grandpa is good at taking hints. He doesn't try to push me into talking if I don't feel like it. I scoot close to him, can smell his aftershave, and we look at the template.

"I think it'll be nice, don't you?" I ask him. I'm nervous I'm going to mess her name up, though. "Maybe you should do all the carving."

"Nah, after I'm done with this part you can practice on one of the spare blocks. You know what? If you slip up a bit, it'll add character. Don't worry about it. The most important part is that she knows you engraved her name yourself, even if it's not perfect. Trust me," he says, squeezing my shoulder.

I nod and we both put on safety glasses. I watch as the etching tool slides through the wood almost like a knife in butter. My grandpa has a steady hand. He's done with the whole picture part in about ten minutes. Then, he hands the engraver over and I practice. It takes me a good half an hour to feel like I can carve it out for real. By the time I turn off the drill, I'm full-on sweating.

"Let's take a look," Grandpa says, brushing the wood chips off. I peel the tracing paper off and am surprised at how great it looks. Then, Grandpa put a different tip on the drill and added in some details, making it look even more three-dimensional. I can't help but grin.

"You did a really fine job, kiddo!" Grandpa says. He sits it down, looking pleased. "Last thing, I bought some light stain. Go grab one of those clean rags out of that drawer. You dip it in the can and rub it on. Simple as that. It'll be dry in about an hour, so you'll have to stay here and hang out with this old geezer," he says. When he reaches for his cane, I see him grimace.

"You OK, Grandpa?" I ask.

He waves his hand like, "yeah, yeah," and starts toward the door that leads to the kitchen.

"Now, do you want me to fry up some ring bologna?" Grandpa asks. That is our big thing to eat together, fried bologna. We're nuts for it.

"Sure, but I can make it if you want me to," I say. "When I'm done with the staining."

He looks at me out of the corner of his eye. His face breaks out in a big smile, like he's been waiting for me to offer.

"Well, all right," he says. "If you insist!" We both laugh.

* * *

AFTER I LEAVE, I notice that Gini sent another song. I listen to it on the way home, stopping on the bridge in Seventh Street Park to see if the turtles are still there. Two grown turtles and a baby have lived in the pond all summer. I didn't see them on the way to Grandpa's so I'm thinking they've already migrated or hibernated or whatever turtles do in the fall. Then, I spot them sunning on a branch that's sticking out of the muddy water. The baby has tripled in size since the spring. It was about the size of a quarter when it was newborn.

Turtles are cool. Something about turtles makes me feel calm. I kind of wish I was a turtle. They don't have to break tough news to their parents or sneak around to be with their girlfriends. Their moms don't move 500 miles away. Their grandpas don't have health problems. Mostly, they can hang out, not a care in the world, all day long. That sounds like a pretty good life to me.

18

MAGIC CARPET RIDE

My head feels buzzy, like the time I drank five Cokes in a row on a dare. I keep thinking, *I can't believe we did it.* It went exactly like we'd planned. Jen went home with her friend Alison after school, so I don't have to worry about her. We all hopped on the public bus from the school parking lot and rode it downtown – me, Gini, Morgan, and Sophie. We got off at the Blake Transit Center. The library is one block east from there.

The only thing that makes me nervous is that it's already 3:45 p.m. and Gini has to be back to the library no later than 5:30 p.m. Her parents are coming to pick her up right at 6 p.m. BUT that leaves nearly two hours to do whatever we want.

"Hey Morgan, Sophie, come here," Gini says, holding her phone up to take a selfie of the three of them in front of the library and quickly texting it to her mom, who asked her to check in when she made it downtown.

"Oh no!" Sophie exclaims, covering her mouth with her hands. Her eyes were wide. I'm learning she's the drama queen of Gini's group and I can tell she is really enjoying being a part of our secret plan. *Maybe she and Anthony should get together,* I think.

"What?!" Gini asks, looking around. "What is it? Is it someone we know?" I can see she's a little shaky. Gini told me that this is the first time she's ever deceived her parents.

Sophie grabs her by both shoulders. "No, but I just thought of something. Do you know if your parents put a tracker on your phone? I have one on mine. My stupid parents won't take it off and they can see every place I go."

UGH! I have a sinking feeling in the pit of my stomach. That is something I hadn't thought about.

"I don't know," Gini says. "How can you tell?"

Both Sophie and Morgan shrug. Gini looks at me. "Do you know how to tell?"

I shake my head no. "We can hang out in the library," I tell her, trying not to sound disappointed, while my heart literally drops into my stomach.

"I don't want you to get caught, G," Sophie says. I can tell she felt bad for bringing it up.

Morgan pulls out her phone and tells us she's going to Google it.

"Now I'm curious if I have a tracker, too," Morgan says. "We could all have trackers!" She takes a pair of glasses out of her hoodie pocket and puts them on. "My contacts are hurting my eyes," she says, looking a little embarrassed, pecking at her phone. "So, it says, basically, that your phone might start acting glitchy if a tracker is on it. Has your phone been shutting off randomly or sending you weird texts? Does it run out of battery super quick? Spyware runs down your battery."

Gini shakes her head no. I feel a little better.

"Mine does all those things! No wonder my phone is so messed up all the time," Sophie says.

"Let me see your phone." Morgan takes it and starts looking through Gini's apps. "I don't see any that look funny, you know, like they don't belong. But you really need to clean these apps up."

"I know," Gini says, taking the phone back. She looks through her apps quickly and says, "I don't think my parents would even know they can put a tracker on my phone, TBH. I think it'll be OK."

"No fair," Sophie says, again. "My parents better take that tracker off, now that I know it's messing up my phone."

I look at Gini and raise my eyebrows. "You sure?" I ask.

"Yes, I'm sure." She smiles shyly at me.

Sophie and Morgan give Gini a long hug, like they'll never see each other again. Then we split off and walk toward State Street. The first stop I have planned for Gini is Graffiti Alley. It's a long alley covered from floor to ceiling with graffiti and there's always something new to see.

"Have you ever been in there?" I ask.

"No, I've only seen it driving by. I did ask my dad if we could check it out, but he says there are too many druggies. Are you sure it's safe to go back in there?"

"Oh yeah," I say. "It's fine. I've been down the alley lots of times, and we won't go around the corner or anything."

Gini nods. I take her hand in mine. "I promise it'll be OK."

As we walk, I point out the places I've been to – Hal's Guitars, Jerusalem Garden, Underground Records.

"Hey," I say, "Not to change the subject, but I was going to say you have some good friends. I thought Morgan and Sophie would be different but they're actually pretty nice. I mean, they were really looking out for you."

"Yeah, that's the thing about having the same besties from, like, preschool, I guess. Well, you know how it is," she says. "You've had the same group of friends forever, too."

I joke that we should set Sophie and Anthony up, and she laughs.

"So, what did you think Sophie and Morgan would be like? Be honest."

"OK, to be honest, I thought you were too good for them because I always thought they kind of acted snobby. Before we started dating, they never paid any attention to me or anyone in my crew. Everyone thinks of your group as the preppy, rich girls who only hang out with the popular rich jocks. Me and my friends are the regular guys, you know?"

"I can see why you'd think that, but they're actually really good friends."

We walked in silence for the next block and then we were at the mouth of the alley. We both pause there, kind of peering around the corner. The alley stretches back about a block and then juts to the right into a space that can't be seen from the road. It is a bit creepy when you get all the way back there. When we start into the alley, I point and say, "See? We don't have to go very far back." I squeeze her hand. "Let's stop here." I pause in front of a big yellow smiley face with Xed-out eyes. "This is a good selfie spot."

"This is exciting," Gini says. I can tell she's really digging it and it makes me see it like it's my first time there, too. "It's kind of like walking into a cave that's had this explosion of color. I love it!" Gini says, twirling in a circle.

Different graffiti artists have covered every inch of the alley. Some only tag while others paint full-on murals. I take out my phone and we snap a couple of pics. Gini kisses me on the cheek in one. These aren't to share, of course. They are only for us.

"It almost makes you feel dizzy. I really love it!" Gini says.

The sun is streaming down through the buildings. In the distance, we can hear the saxophone player who always seems to be standing on the corner of Maynard and Liberty with his instrument case open for donations. He's playing a slow, romantic-sounding song.

"It sounds like the kind of song my parents used to slow dance to," I tell Gini. "Can you hear that?"

"Yes, let's dance! Come on!" she says, grabbing my hand and running toward the back of the alley. I breathe a little quicker, wondering if this is our *chance*. I've been wanting to kiss her for days on end!

When we get to the end of the alley, where it turns to the right, we peek to see if anyone's hanging out back there. There's only one couple standing near the back entry to a restaurant. They're smoking and talking quietly but passionately about something, so they don't even notice us as we continue around the corner. When they turn to flick their cigarettes into the alley, I see they're wearing Tios Mexican Restaurant shirts.

"Hey! That's my family's favorite restaurant," I call out to them. "We love Tios!"

"That's cool," the guy comments, giving me a thumbs up. Then they disappear into the back door to the restaurant, and we have the whole alley to ourselves.

OK, get it together. It's time to go for it, I tell myself, trying to get the nerve to make my move.

"Do you know how to slow dance?" Gini asks.

"I don't have the slightest clue."

She laughs.

"Let's try," I say. "I think you put your hands around my neck, like this." I take her hands and put them around my neck. "And then I put my hands on, um, here." I very slightly rest my hands near her hips. We start to sway, a little, like I've seen my parents do, dancing in the kitchen.

Gini's waist feels so tiny. We're about the same height and we grin at each other for a minute. Then, Gini rests her head on my shoulder. We twirl a few more times around. I try to dip her, but it takes her by surprise, and she starts giggling. Suddenly, she lifts her face toward mine and our lips are touching.

It's like an explosion goes off in my head. It's happening. It's happening. I feel light-headed and, for some reason, so relieved I feel tears in my eyes.

I was worried all day that it would be either too wet a kiss or too dry, or that I'd do something awkward, like bonk noses. I Googled all the ways you can mess up a first kiss and it's nothing like the cringy videos I'd watched.

Gini's lips are soft. We stay that way, for a few long seconds, and my whole body is tingly. She pulls away first. For a second, I'm worried she's upset, but she looks happy.

There are people coming into the alley now. We can hear them talking and walking toward the back of the alley, where we are still standing super close. Both of my arms are wrapped around her waist now. Gini kisses me again, quickly, before we split apart.

"We better get going, I suppose," she says, taking my hand. We start back toward the entryway.

The people walking toward us look like an old hippie couple, and the long gray-haired lady is looking at us all dopey-eyed. They smell like incense from the weed shop down the block. "Aw, aren't they cute, Ger?" the lady comments, as if we aren't walking by.

When they're out of earshot, I whisper, "I'll give you cute, lady," which, for some reason, cracks us both up. We laugh all the way out of the alley.

One block up is my favorite coffee shop in Ann Arbor. We stop there, and Gini orders a frozen mocha.

"I'll have the same thing," I tell the guy behind the corner. "Nice Mohawk, by the way."

"Thanks, dude!" he smiles.

I take out my wallet. This is the first time I've ever used it. I feel both older and a little silly until I look at Gini and see she's smiling non-stop, which makes me smile. I'm sure we look like a couple of grinning goofballs, but I do not care!

I walk her over to the fireplace and we get lucky to find a table nearby, away from the windows, in case anyone we know might be strolling downtown. I'm feeling pretty darn proud that the date is working out so well. In fact, I don't think I've ever felt so sure of myself as I do right now. I've kissed a girl and not just any girl, but *THE GIRL* I happen to like a lot. I can't wait to tell Lamar.

"I want to know about your rabbit. I think that's so neat! Amma and Daddy won't even let us get a hamster. *No pets,*" she says, mimicking her mom. I laugh. "Mabel, she lives with you, like a cat?"

"Yeah, rabbits are a lot like cats. People don't know that. We have two, but Mabel was the smarter of the two, so she does all the shows. The other one is lazy but Han keeps Mabel company. He's kind of a dork."

Gini is smiling while she takes a big spoonful of her drink. "So, this is a weird question, but do they go outside to do you-know-what?"

"No, they have a litter box."

"Really? Just like a cat? No way!"

"Yeah, we got Mabel and Han from this really cool rabbit sanctuary out in the country. They also rescue potbelly pigs. When I went there, I walked into the house and there's this lumpy blanket on the couch that started moving. It was a pig about the size of a bulldog."

Gini laughs. "I would have been so freaked out," she says. "But that's so cool."

"Yeah, the lady who runs the place is really nice. She told us all about rabbits. They're pack animals. They need to be around other rabbits, or they get depressed, and they love getting petted, if you train them right."

"Really? I didn't know that! Who got to name them?"

"Jen got to name the girl and I named the boy."

"Han? Isn't that German?" We're both laughing now.

"I know, it's a funny name for a bunny, but I was really into Star Wars when we got them. You know Han Solo?"

She nods. "So, why are you thinking of quitting doing magic? You're really talented."

She puts her hand on my arm when she says that. I feel my cheeks turning red. My heart rate was starting to get back to normal from our kiss and now it's off to the races again. I try to pretend I'm not thinking about the kiss, even though it keeps replaying in my brain.

"I've been practicing to try out for the basketball team. I don't know if I'll get on, but I at least want to try, and that will take a lot of my free time. Plus, we've been doing the same show over and over every weekend. It's gotten boring. I mean, he's trying to change it up a bit with some lasers, but it's all his ideas. He never goes with my ideas."

"Have you tried to do your own tricks? Things that you think are cool?"

I thought back to when I'd mentioned to my dad about wearing a different outfit. "I don't know," I say. "I've sort of tried that."

"Are you afraid your dad might be hurt if you tell him you want to quit? 'Cause that's really hard. I know I don't like disappointing my parents."

"Um, yeah. For sure, that's part of it. Now my dad's got us all signed up to do the Thanksgiving Talent Show. I'm, like, totally dreading it. I know I need to tell him."

Gini looks me in the eyes and puts her hand on mine. I look out the window before continuing.

"My dad's been acting different since my mom put this plan together to go to Iowa. I think he's depressed, and he tries hard not to show it. He loves doing the shows with me, like, more than anything. I guess I'm scared it would really mess him up to have me quit. I keep wimping out on telling him I'm grown now. I want to do my own things my own way, you know?"

"Oh, trust me, I get it," Gini said. "What if you started doing your own shows?"

"I don't know. It's hard to come up with new tricks that work. I've tried a couple times–"

"Show me," she interrupts. "I'd like to see then some time."

I nod and then I look at my phone and see that it's already 4:25. I can't believe it. We only have a little over an hour left and it will take at least 10 minutes to get all the way over to our next stop.

"We should get going," I say, and she nods, standing up and putting her jacket on. It is a bit chillier when we walk outside, and the sky is getting cloudy. I debate changing the plan for a split second and then decide that we can make it if we hurry.

"Did you know that you can watch the UM Marching Band practice every Friday night?" I ask. "They actually have bleachers set up and go through the whole routine they're going to do at the game tomorrow. It's a few blocks. Do you want to go watch?"

Gini claps her hands like a cheerleader. "Are you serious? That is so awesome. Definitely! Which way is it?" She grabs my hand.

I feel giddy, walking with her through town!

On the way, I show her all the places I know, naming them off as we stroll by, like a tour guide. If she already knows what they are, she doesn't say anything. I tell her, "There's the art museum, the archeology museum where they have all these mummies. That's the Michigan Union and, across the street, is the Law Quad."

We walk past Pizza Bob's, and I ask her if she wants a slice, but she says she is full from her frozen mocha. I can tell she is very impressed that I know all these places.

We hear the music way before we get to the band practice field. The majorette is yelling instructions about where the tubas need to be standing and waving her hands in the air, making motions I don't understand. We take a seat in the bleachers, our legs touching. I look at Gini and she's staring straight ahead, watching the band practice, or pretending to.

I put my hand on her leg. She looks at me then, and smiles.

"Pretty cool, huh?" I say.

"It is really cool!"

Full confession, with my hand on her knee, I can't focus on the band. I have no idea what they're playing. I sit there in a spacey daze. After a few songs, I lean over and say, "I have one more thing I want you to see." I don't really have any more stops planned. I just desperately want to find a place where we can kiss some more. Gini nods and smiles.

"Let's go, then!" she says.

19
MISDIRECTION

The park where the band practices is about five blocks from the library. Right across the street from the park is a huge lumber yard and store. There are stacks and stacks of lumber. I look around for a place we can sneak over to and do some smooching. I also want to give her the present Grandpa and I made, too. I'm hoping we can find someplace a little private.

I am getting paranoid because my hands are getting sweaty. I pause and pull my hand away to wipe them on my pants. "I'm sorry. My hands are getting sweaty."

"I was worried about my hands being sweaty," she says, laughing. "What time is it, by the way?"

We totally haven't been keeping track. I pull out my phone and can't believe it when I see it's half past 5. That was the time I wanted to get her back to the library, to be safe. I tell Gini the time and her eyes grow big as saucers.

"Oh no! We better get back to the library, OK?" she asks.

"Um, but there's something–"

"I don't think we can do another stop," she interrupts. I can hear the nervousness in her voice.

I consider taking the gift out and giving it to her then, but I can see plain as day she is agitated. This isn't how I imagined it would go. Gini starts speed-walking toward Liberty Street.

I have to jog to catch up. We are practically running as we turn to go the last two blocks when Gini suddenly stops dead in her tracks. I see this horrified look on her face.

"What's wrong?" I whisper. My heart feels like it's in my throat.

"Is that my parents' car?" She points to a blue van parked slightly crooked in the street. Gini abruptly turns around and starts walking back the way we came.

"Gini, where are you going?" I whisper-shout. "Is there anyone in the van?"

"I don't know. I can't see," Gini whispers back. "Oh my God, I can't look!" She stops walking and turns her head slightly, so her hair is covering part of her face. Her cheeks are blazing red. "I should have predicted they'd come early! What was I thinking?"

I walk up to her and put my hand on her shoulder. She takes a deep breath and hangs her head. I can tell she's on the verge of crying.

"Stay here," I tell her. "I'll go look." It is all I can think to do.

"My brother always keeps a bin of Hot Wheels in the back-seat. That's how you can tell if it's our car."

I cross the street, keeping my eyes on the van. I don't see any movement and, once I get closer, I can see no one is there.

Please don't be their car, I pray. *Please, God, I'll do anything!*

My heart sinks into my Adidas. The Hot Wheels are there. I'm going to have to break the news to her. Her parents are in the library.

I spin around and see that Gini is hiding behind the statue near the driveway to the funeral home across the street. I wave her over.

"I think this is your van," I tell her as soon as she crosses the street. Gini looks inside and nods her head, grimly. I've never seen her look so depressed.

"They must be inside already, probably looking all over the place for me." Her voice is shaking. She holds up her phone and I see it's out of power. "Morgan and Sophie are probably text bombing me as we speak. I have no idea how long it's been out of charge. Oh my God, this is bad!"

"That's right!" I say, trying to sound upbeat. "Morgan and Sophie are there. They were going to put them off if something like this happened. Like, tell them you're in the bathroom. That kind of thing? I'm sure they're totally covering for you."

We had sort of talked about this type of scenario on the bus, but I can't remember what we decided they should say. I start to wonder why I ever thought this date was a good idea in the first place. It might go down as the worst date in Ann Arbor history.

Gini shakes her head. "I don't know," she says, taking another deep breath. I can see tears in her eyes and can tell she's trying to hold it together.

"I'm dead. I'm going to be grounded for a year." She's talking super-fast. "An ENTIRE year! Plus, they might not ever let me go out with my friends again. They will never let me see you." Now tears are streaming down her face. "I don't know what to do."

My heart is beating fast, thinking about her parents confronting me or, worse, making sure Gini and I break up. I take her hand, but I don't know what to say. I'm feeling super fidgety, so I pull my phone out and see that it's now 5:45 p.m. I might throw up.

I thought we had a rock-solid plan. I blew it!

"I'm so sorry, Gini," I say. *Ugh, lame.*

"I better go," she says and drops my sweaty hand. She starts walking slowly toward the library. I feel a lump in my throat, watching her.

"Gini," I yell, running to catch up. "Wait, what are you going to say? Do you want me to come in the library with you? I can tell them this was all my idea, that it's my fault and that I pressured you into it, or something. I'll say anything..."

Gini shakes her head no. "That's not a good idea. Don't worry. I'll think of something. Just go and I'll text you later, k?" She's trying to be so sweet, which makes me feel so much worse.

Gini turns and I watch her walk quickly toward the entrance. She pauses for a minute at the glass doors before walking in. *It'll be a miracle if she wants to be my girlfriend after this*, I think. Then she disappears inside.

I feel frozen in place, staring at the library building. It's killing me not knowing what's happening to her. I think about running in. I know she's in deep trouble, from the sounds of it. I couldn't care less if I get in trouble with them or my parents. I can take the heat. I mean, my parents have pretty much screwed up my whole life, my mom by leaving and my dad constantly pressuring me about the shows.

But Gini's parents trusted her. She told me that and I talked her into this great big lie. Now that might be totally blown and it's all my fault. *My* reputation will be ruined, in their eyes. I doubt they'll ever let me date Gini, officially, now. We'll have to sneak around the entire rest of the school year and all through high school until we're, like, 18 and can do whatever we want.

I take my phone out to text her. I start to ask what's happening and then erase it.

Should I come in?

I erase that one, too, remembering that her phone is dead.

After a few seconds, I turn and start walking away from the library. The sun is setting as I head west toward home. This is usually my favorite part of the day, with the sky all lit up behind the city, all oranges, purples, and reds. But it doesn't even touch me; that's how down I feel.

All I can do is pray, over and over, that everything with Gini will be the same, that we'll see each other in school on Monday and go right back to what we had. I need that. I need everything with us to stay the same, so I pray all the way home: *"God, please, I'm begging, don't let Gini get in trouble. Don't let her parents hate me. Please!"*

20
ABRA-CADAVER

It takes 20 minutes to walk from downtown to our house, so it's nearly 6:30 when I walk through the back door. Dad and Jen are already sitting at the table, eating dinner.

"Oh good," Dad says. "We just started."

He motions to the pot on the stove. Spaghetti again. Jen only likes spaghetti, tacos, mac and cheese, chicken legs, and grilled steak. I'd complain but I know what Dad would say: "Feel free to start cooking more, then!"

"Where ya been?" Jen raises one eyebrow at me, like she's suspicious about something. She knows that look gets my goat and I'm NOT in the mood. When Dad isn't looking, I stick my tongue out at her. Jen laughs so hard that some noodles and sauce comes flying out of her mouth. Dad looks confused, which only makes her laugh harder.

"All right, you two." He points his fork at Jen and then at me. "Jay, get your plate and come sit down. We're out of parmesan, but you can throw some of that shredded cheddar cheese on the spaghetti and microwave it for about 30 seconds. Warm those green beans up, too." He points to an open can on the counter.

"Put those in a bowl first. If you put metal of any kind in a microwave, you'll scorch it."

"I know how to microwave things," I say. It comes out a lot crappier than I'd intended. Dad looks confused, but he lets it go.

"I'm starving," he goes on. "Been trying to diet all week. Get rid of this belly." He pats his stomach.

Jen reaches over and pokes his tummy. "But I like your belly, Daddy. It's my pillow. I don't want you to lose weight. I like you exactly how you are."

He smiles at her. "That's sweet, hon. Now sit, Jay, please, and eat something."

"I'm not very hungry," I say. "Mind if I go to my room?"

"Did you get something to eat already?"

"No, I'm not hungry, that's all." I lean up against the counter. The kitchen is a mess. Dad always destroys the kitchen when he cooks. I hope he doesn't expect me to clean it up. I know that's one of the things that irritates my mom a lot – his constant messiness. I can see her point. I REALLY want to go to my room and text Gini and Lamar. I feel agitated and I wish he'd let me do what I want, for once. *Is it too much to ask to skip dinner?*

"I want you to eat a little something," he says.

"Fine." I grab the plate he's sat out for me and scoop a tiny amount of noodles out of the pot, and then ladle an equally small amount of sauce on top. I sit down at the table, pull out my phone and check to see if Gini has sent me any messages. Nothing.

"Not going to warm it up?" Dad asks. "Here, I'll warm it up for you."

"It's fine," I say, setting the phone on the table kind of hard.

"You OK?" he asks.

"Yeah, I'm fine."

We eat in silence for a few minutes. That's rare for our house. Jen keeps looking at us, worried. I stare at my phone, trying to telepathically will it to ding with a message from Gini saying everything's fine.

"Hey, what do you call a dead magician?" Dad asks. I know he's really trying, so I play along.

"I don't know, Dad, what do you call a dead magician?"

Dad pauses for effect. "Abra-cadaver." Dad beams.

"I don't get it. What's a cadaver?" Jen asks.

"It's a dead person," Dad says. "I thought you'd know what a cadaver is."

Jen laughs and I groan.

"Well, that went over like a lead balloon. So, what's the plan for the weekend, Jay? Any big dates?" Dad tries to joke again. *Always joking.* I ignore him. I haven't told him about Gini or about our date downtown. I wonder if Grandpa said anything about Gini and the gift. Thinking about Gini's gift, still sitting in my backpack, makes me feel even more down. Suddenly, my stomach feels sour. I sit the fork down and push my plate away.

"OK, not in the mood to talk, I see," Dad continues, while I try hard not to let on about my queasy stomach. "Well, let me tell you what I have going on. Tomorrow, I'm going to your grandfather's to see what we need to do to make the house more handicap friendly." He pauses a minute, putting his fork down. Dad sighs loudly and his demeanor shifts.

Sometimes, I can tell when there's a big announcement coming. I watch him, waiting, my heart starting to pound. *Is this it? Is this the day we find out they're getting divorced?*

"Speaking of Grandpa, there's something I have to tell you both." Dad gets up as he's talking and scraps his half-eaten plate of food into the trash. *I thought he said he was starving. It must be something serious. Not about divorce, but serious.*

"What's going on with Grandpa?" I ask.

Dad looks at me, almost surprised I'd been paying attention. He leans on the island with his elbows and looks back and forth between me and Jen. "I don't want you to get upset but there's no easy way to say this. You know how Grandpa has had diabetes for many years now and you might have seen him limping. It's his right leg. He's got a bad infection and the best thing they can do for him is take the leg. He'll get a prosthetic and every–"

"Wait! What?"

Dad looks at me. I can see tears springing into his eyes. He nods and says, "Grandpa has to get his right leg amputated, kiddo. They've done all they can, otherwise. Luckily, we live by a wonderful hospital."

I look at him and start to feel light-headed. Jen stops chewing, then spits a mouthful of green beans onto her plate.

"What do you mean?" I ask. "Why?" *Did Grandpa know when I'd gone over to make the gift? How could he not mention that? How is he going to walk?*

"Like I said, that's what happens to some people with diabetes. This happens, sometimes." I could feel tears welling. I can't even tell anymore if I feel angry or sad.

"No!" Jen yells and starts crying.

"Jen, hon, it'll be OK. I promise," Dad says, gently grabbing her by the arm and pulling her out of her chair. She curls up on his lap. For a minute, I think she might stick her thumb in her mouth. It took her years to get over that habit. I can tell she's thinking about it. She starts biting her nails instead.

"When? Does that mean Mom's coming home?" Maybe that would, at least, be a silver lining. She's going to have to come home now. Who else will take care of him? Maybe things will go back to how they were before she got the stupid idea to get her master's degree.

"It's scheduled for next Friday, literally right in the middle of your mom's mid-terms. She'll be home in a month. Grandpa is coming to stay here for a few weeks, at least, and maybe longer. We'll see." He rubs Jen's back. *How can he be so calm about that? How is anything Mom is doing OK with him?*

"Are you serious? She's not coming for the surgery? It's her dad!"

They both look startled, like I'm the one acting strange. I stand up fast and the back of the chair bangs against the China cabinet behind me. Dishes rattle.

"What a bunch of crap!" I yell. "I hate her! I literally hate her!"

"Hey!" my dad yells.

Jen hops off his lap and runs toward the hallway. She slams her bedroom door so hard the dishes rattle again.

"Jesus, Jay, don't say that. I mean it. Do not ever say that again," Dad says, his teeth clenched. I know I've done it now. I've never seen him that angry with me.

We stare at each other, him glaring at me and me glaring back. I have this sinking feeling, like we might never be the same. Not the two of us, not our family.

This is what a broken family feels like, I think. I do feel broken, for him and for Jen, mostly. What did they do to deserve this? I hate her right now. I can't imagine ever forgiving her. Tears stream down my face.

Dad's face changes. "Oh Jayster," he says, his voice cracking. I look away, afraid he might start crying. "Come on. Give your mom a break. Let's all lighten up a bit, OK? Mom is coming back in less than four weeks and your grandpa will be all right. I promise. He's the toughest old dude I know."

He stands up and opens his arms for me to come in for a hug, but I stay put. He lowers his arms. I want to believe him but saying something's going to happen and seeing it happen are two different things. I get that sinking feeling again. I have to get out.

"I want to stay at Lamar's for the weekend," I tell him, wiping my face off on the arm of my hoodie.

"Really? I was hoping you would stay here for this one weekend. You've been gone a lot, Jay. Pretty much every weekend.

We miss ya. Tomorrow night, we could take Grandpa to the movies. Wouldn't that be fun?"

I really don't want to be at our house. It doesn't feel like my home anymore, anyway. I thought the day Mom left was bad, but this is the worst day of my life. First Gini getting caught for something I talked her into doing, then Grandpa's surgery, and then hearing about yet another of my mom's stupid, selfish decisions. I feel like my brain might explode if I have to deal with one more thing. I want to go to Lamar's and have his mom cook for us, play video games with his dad, throw some hoops, and NOT think of any of this crap.

"Fine," Dad says, giving in, "that's fine." He starts to clear the dishes from the table. "But I want you home tomorrow night, no later than 9 p.m. We have a gig Sunday morning down at the Methodist Church. I'm sorry I forgot to mention it sooner. It's been a crazy week."

I can't believe it. The day before basketball tryouts. I need that time to practice.

"No," I say before I can stop myself. "I don't want to do a gig Sunday."

"What?"

"Maybe I don't want to do the show Sunday. I mean, is that OK with you?" I know I sounded bratty again. It's like I can't help it, being a jerk.

"No, son, actually it's not." Dad turns the water off and looks at me with that stupid, confused look on his face again. *How can he possibly not know I'm sick and tired of the magic shows?*

"And I don't particularly like the way you're talking to me," he adds. "If you want to start doing fewer shows, we can discuss it. The way you're acting, though, is unacceptable."

"Oh, OK," I spit out, sarcastically. "You and Mom get to do whatever you want. She takes off for two years and everyone acts like that's normal. And you have your magic. I mean, you might love doing the shows, Dad, but I don't. Apparently, I can't do anything I want. I mean, what the hell?"

Dad throws his plate into the sink, breaking it. "Hey, mister, you watch your mouth! You're really pushing it tonight," he says, throwing a dish towel on the counter.

We stare at each other for a minute. Then he says, "Look, I know this news about your grandpa is upsetting. I know your mom being gone is upsetting. But I'm confused about the magic. You used to love doing the shows. It's something we can do together, the two of us. That's the best part for me, you know?"

I can't stand hearing him sound so pitiful, like the night Mom told him about Iowa. Sometimes I wish he would let himself stay mad – yell and scream his guts out. I look away from the hurt in his eyes.

I can't deal with this, I think, picking up my phone and starting toward the door. *I need to leave before I say something I regret.*

"Bud?"

I stop and say, "I'm going to Lamar's now. OK, Dad?"

He puts the dishes down and wipes his hands off.

"I think we need to talk," he says, motioning toward the table. "Plus, your mom is hoping to Zoom with you and Jen tonight. She is very worried about Grandpa and the two of you, you know?"

"Can I please go to Lamar's now?" I'm on the verge of crying again.

Dad stares at me for another minute. He takes a deep breath.

"Please?" I ask. "I'll be back tomorrow night so we can do the show. I'll call Mom Sunday and do the show. Dad, *please?*"

As soon as he nods, I take off. I don't even pack a bag. They always have an extra toothbrush. They're an extra toothbrush kind of family.

* * *

I SPILL my guts to Lamar and then stay up until three in the morning hoping Gini will send me a message. All I can think of is that we've been found out and her parents must have taken her phone away from her. And because it's the weekend, I'll have to wait until Monday to find out what happened. This entire weekend is going to be torture. Pure torture.

21
MAGICAL MISFIRES

I wake up around 10 a.m. to a slew of DMs on Snapchat. Both Sophie and Morgan messaged me, basically describing the same thing, how Gini's parents showed up at the library early and how they tried to stall them by telling them Gini was off looking for a specific kind of book for her homework. How her parents panicked when Sophie and Morgan finally had to spill the beans about what we were all up to. How Gini started crying the minute she saw her parents standing there waiting for her. Morgan heard her mother say "for shame" under her breath. Then they all left. They said it was complete silence all the way home. They were dropped off at Morgan's and they haven't heard a peep from Gini ever since. They were wondering if she'd messaged me. I DMed back.

> No, she hasn't. I wish...

They shot off a bunch of sad emojis. I'm pacing by the time Lamar wakes up.

"What's up, bro?"

"It's really bad," I tell him.

"What's going on?"

I notice Lamar is suddenly shy about standing up in his underwear. He jiggles into his pants under his blankets before getting out of bed. Is everything going to be weird from now on? That's how it's starting to feel. I try to ignore that odd little thing he did.

"Gini's in big trouble and it's all my fault," I say.

"Did you hear from her?" he asks.

"No, but Sophie and Morgan DMed me." I tell him everything about what they said.

"Do you think we should ride our bikes out to her house?" I ask.

Lamar scratches his head and stares at me for a minute. "What would you do if we did?"

I try to envision walking up to her door, knocking, her parents answering. *What would I say?*

"Can't we just go, and I'll think about it on the way?"

"Sure, I'll go with you, bro. But what if it makes things worse for you and Gini? You don't know what she told them. What if you say something that gets her in even more hot water?"

I take a deep breath and close my eyes. I know he's probably right, but I can't sit there doing nothing while Gini is home under quarantine.

Lamar walks over to the window and pulls up the shade. "It's raining, so that plan is out any way. You'd have to talk your dad into driving us over there."

"Or my grandpa," I say, without thinking. Then it hits me. I can't ask him for another favor when he's going through so much. He might not even be able to drive. I should be the one helping him out.

"Yeah, he'd do it," Lamar says.

"No, never mind." I sigh.

"Why not? He'd probably have some good advice about the

whole situation. Plus, he already knows about Gini. You know he'd do anything for you."

I suddenly feel super guilty. I'd been so obsessed with the Gini situation, I'd kind of forgotten about my grandpa. I sink into Lamar's gaming chair, put my face in my hands. "God, why am I screwing up so much?" I mumble.

"Dude, what's going on?" Lamar sits on his bed. I can tell by his tone of voice that he is genuinely worried about me.

"I can't ask him for anything right now because he's kind of going through a big thing," I say, looking at Lamar. "He has to get one of his legs amputated."

The thought of it makes me woozy. What if he dies during the surgery? And I'd been so wrecked about Gini, I hadn't even bothered to mention it to Lamar last night.

"Dude, that's messed up," Lamar says. Lamar has known my grandparents since we were three. He's been over to their house a lot, playing card games with my grandma and hammering nails out in the workshop with my grandpa. He cried harder than I did at Grandma's funeral.

"Why does this crap always happen to the best people?" Lamar says, sadly. "I mean, losing your grandma and now this? He doesn't deserve it."

"I know," I say, picking up my phone. I honestly don't want to think or talk about it. Plus, I keep hoping I'll suddenly get a message from Gini. Again, there's nothing. I scroll through Snapchat to see if anyone else mentioned the situation at the library. I wouldn't want it getting around, what we did, for Gini's sake. I don't want anyone but our friends knowing that we'd snuck around town together and got caught, big time.

Luckily, there's no mention of it. I text Morgan and Sophie to make sure they don't tell anyone about it. I ask them if they think I should go to Gini's house and they both, right away, text:

NO!

So, that was that.

"You know what?" Lamar says, looking up from his phone. "We should go check on your grandpa today. We're not going to be able to get any practice in outside. Just look at the weather. It's gonna rain all day. Maybe we could meet up with Anthony and Sal at the Y later."

"Yeah, that's a great idea," I say, absentmindedly. "You wouldn't mind going over there with me?"

"Nah, dude, 'course not. But can you text Anthony? He's been acting weird."

That made me look up. Lamar is sitting crossed legged. His glasses are hanging down almost to the end of his nose. He looks like a worried professor. I know exactly what he's thinking.

"What do you mean? How's he been acting?" I am instantly angry. If Anthony is going to go cold on Lamar for being gay, after eight years of being friends with us, then he can seriously take a hike.

"I don't know. He's been off." Lamar tries to sound all casual, but I can tell he is really bothered. "I mean, have you heard from him much lately?"

Now that Lamar says it, I realize I haven't been hearing from him. It dawns on me that he hasn't called a crew meeting in, like, at least two weeks.

I shoot him a text immediately.

> What's up, bro? Want to get some b-ball time in at the Y with me and Lamar later?

I set my phone down to run to the bathroom to take a leak. I hear it ding a few seconds later and pick it up. It's a message from my dad:

> Need you home, bud. Come straight home when you get this. Cooking fried egg sandwiches for lunch.

"Aw, man! My dad wants me to come straight home. Last night, he said I could stay until late. Let me see if I can get out of it."

> Going with Lamar to see Grandpa. Then meeting friends at Y.

> No. Come. Home.

I slam my phone down on the couch.

"Gotta go?" asks Lamar.

"Yeah," I say right as another DM comes in. It's from Anthony:

> Can't today, dude. Lots going on.

"That's weird," I say. "Since when does Anthony have a lot going on?"

Lamar laughs. "Don't sweat it. It's really not a big deal."

"Did you tell him that you're gay?"

"Yeah, not long after I told you, I also told Drake and Sal. I didn't want them to find out from somebody else, you know?"

I don't know what possesses me, but without thinking, I call Anthony straight up.

"Yeah," he says, startled. "What's up? Why you calling me?"

"Nothing's up with me," I say. "We're wondering what's up with you."

"Who's we?" he asks.

"Me and Lamar."

There's a pause. Then he says, "Nothing's wrong. I've been busy, that's all."

I look at Lamar, who is watching me like a hawk. I can tell he's uncomfortable.

"I want to know, straight up, are you ditching us or what? I mean, suddenly, you start acting weird. Don't even want to be around me. Or around Lamar. Are you, like, are you homophobic or something?"

Lamar flinches a little at that.

"Really?!" Anthony shouts. "That's where you're going with this? Come on, man. You should know better than that."

I am legit surprised by his answer. He didn't hem and haw like I thought he would. I smile and give Lamar the a-OK sign.

"Well, then, what's been up with you?" Now I feel a bit bad flat-out accusing him.

"You owe me an apology," says Anthony. "I don't think any different about Lamar. He's still one of my best friends. That really sucks, you thinking I'd turn my back on him."

"You're right," I say. "I'm sorry, dude. I guess I'm in a bad mood. There's a lot going on."

Anthony is quiet for a minute.

"Yeah, I get it. Don't worry. Maybe we can all get together tomorrow."

"I'm doing a show with my dad at Grandpa's church, but I'll be home after noon."

"OK, I'll check with Sal and you check with Lamar. Maybe 2 p.m. at Lamar's?"

"Sounds good, dude. And I really am sorry."

"That's OK. Gotta go."

"Wait," I say. "What has been up with you? Something wrong?"

"Um..." He pauses for a long time.

"Just tell me," I push.

"It's not that big a deal, man. I'm not going out for basketball anymore. I'm gonna try out for theater."

"What?!"

"What's going on?" Lamar mouths to me. He's sitting close.

"Hey, dude, I'm gonna put you on speaker so Lamar can talk, too. That OK?"

"Sure, I guess. May as well get this over with."

"Hey bro!" Lamar says. "What's this about basketball? You know we need you on defense."

"Yeah, I know. That's why I haven't been around much. I do have something to confess to you, Lamar." We can hear Anthony's breathing hard, like he's super nervous or something. Lamar and I are looking at each other on pins and needles. *"WTH?"* Lamar mouths.

"Um, OK," Lamar says, mouthing the word *"drama"* to me.

"So, about two weeks ago, when we were having that planning sesh to get Jay out of the talent show, I sort of ran into your sister upstairs."

"You 'ran' into Lydia in her own house two weeks ago." I use air quotes and Lamar has to cover his mouth to stop from laughing.

"Yeah, so…the thing is, Lamar, I've had a crush on your sister for, like, a year now. I am so sorry, man, that I kept it from you. I was embarrassed and I never, in a million years, thought she'd be into me. So, I figured it didn't matter, anyway."

"Do not tell me you and Lydia are going out!" Lamar says, his mouth hanging open. "Come on, spill it already!"

Lamar and I are practically crying by this point, trying to stifle our laughing. I, super quick, put the phone on mute and we both burst out laughing, rolling on his bed. Lamar was banging his hand on the bed. I buried my face in his pillow. Did Anthony seriously think we were totally stupid? We've known about the crush the whole time. The thought of Anthony and Lydia together – total giggling fit.

Anthony takes a long breath and then says, "Well, I'm up in the kitchen and your sister walks in. She's wearing a crop top and those cutoff jeans…"

"Whoa, whoa, whoa," Lamar says. "Dude, we don't need those kinda deets! Come on, man!"

"OK, OK. We like each other. There. That's it, basically. We've been boyfriend and girlfriend for two weeks now."

"Wait a minute," I say. "Back up to the kitchen part again. What exactly happened? Inquiring minds want to know."

"Lamar?" Anthony says.

"Yeah, OK, you can tell us."

"So, basically, she walks in and, like, walks straight up to me and says she likes me, too, and that she has liked me for a while, and we may as well go out. Then, she, like, kissed me on the lips really fast and walked away."

"WHAT?!?!" I screech. "DUDE, THAT IS CRAZY!"

Lamar is sitting with his head in his hands. "I don't even know what to think about that," he says, "but I really don't need to know all the deets. I'm happy for you, bro. You don't have to keep that a secret anymore. I'm cool with it."

"Really? Dude, that is such a relief!" Anthony is gushing now, sounding like his old self. "I mean, it's been really tough not having you guys to talk to about all of this. Wow, what a relief!"

"But what about basketball?" Lamar asks.

"Yeah, I'm not trying out. I'm sorry. I was talking with Lydia and telling her that I'm, like, kinda tired of playing sports all year around. I'd never give up football. You know that's my main thing. I don't know yet about baseball but I'm not doing basketball. I'm going to try out for the musical, actually. I know my voice sucks, but Lydia says she thinks I can get in the chorale, whatever that is, and they're doing *The Addams Family*. Your sister, like, you know, has a voice like an angel. I totally trust her judgement. I'm still super nervous about auditioning, though. You probably both think I'm crazy for doing this."

"Actually," I say, "I can see it. You've always been a drama king." I tease, but I mean it. Anthony will probably do all right in drama.

"We can come to the audition and cheer you on," Lamar says. I'm not sure if he's kidding or serious.

"No, absolutely not! And don't tell Drake yet, or anybody else. I'm gonna tell Sal, in my own time but I only want you two to know for now. OK?"

"Of course," I say. "And, hey, thanks for typing up that list for me. I don't think I ever thanked you for the 'get out of magic show' list you put together."

"Yeah, what's going on with that, Jay? I mean, some of the ideas we came up with are pretty silly. Maybe you ought to just spill the beans to your dad, you know? Tell him straight up."

"Well, I sorta tried to last night and he told me the best part of doing magic is that we get to do it together. So, yeah. Guilt City!"

Neither of them says anything. Lamar gives me a sad smile. I know they both feel bad about everything. My phone dings again. It's my dad wondering what's taking me so long.

"Hey, bro, I'm glad you told us all of this but I gotta go. My dad needs me home for whatever reason."

"No prob!" Anthony says. He sounds a lot happier – almost giddy, really. Must be nice. My heart sinks, again, thinking about what's going on with Gini. I'm glad Anthony didn't ask about our date. I really didn't feel like getting into it right then.

"Hey, Lamar," Anthony continues, sounding more serious than I've ever heard him.

Maybe it's that his voice has dropped. "I want you to know that I will treat your sister like the queen she is. I solemnly swear to be the best boyfriend in history."

Lamar has taken his pillow and covered his entire face with it. His whole body is shaking with laughter.

"You better, or I swear you will pay," Lamar says, trying to sound all serious, but his voice comes out squeaky. The pillow is shaking; he's laughing so hard.

"You got my solemn vow, bro," Anthony says, super seriously.

"Cool, bye," I manage to say before I hang up and we both totally lose it.

When we finally calm down, Lamar says, "He better not try any funny business with my sister, or I'll..." He hits his pillow with his fist a couple times. That sends us laughing again. Then, we take a few selfies and shoot them to Anthony – Lamar and I duck-facing and a couple of other goofy snaps. With everything going on, I really needed that.

22
OPEN SESAME

I walk in and am hoping to slide into my room without Dad seeing me but he's sitting at the kitchen counter. He looks like hell warmed over. His eyes are bloodshot, and he has huge, dark bags under his eyes. I take my jacket off and hang it up.

"Can I have some coffee?" I ask, motioning to the full pot.

"Sure, help yourself," he says. "Grab a mug out of the dishwasher. They're clean."

I like my coffee with five sugar cubes and a big splash of cream. Dad usually teases me, saying, "Why don't you have some coffee with your sugar?" Today, he says nothing.

I sit down at the table and ask, "You OK?"

"Not really," he says, rubbing his forehead. "I didn't get a ton of sleep last night. I'm worried my reactions are making you even more angry at your mom than you would have been."

"Bull!" I yell, hitting the counter with my hand. "Quit blaming yourself, Dad! She's the one being selfish, not you. You're here taking care of everyone and everything. You're even taking care of *her dad*!"

"Your grandpa has been more of a dad to me than my father

ever was, right from the get-go. I don't even see him as a father-in-law," he says. "He's helped me out a ton over the years. I don't think of it like I'm helping *her* dad."

I nod because I know that's true. Dad's been honest about his father. I've only met my Grandpa Dean twice in my whole life. He left my dad and his brother when they were, like, eight and eleven and only popped in now and then. He drank a lot and didn't ever give them money or help them out. My Grandma Joyce did everything. She raised them all by herself. I wish I could have known her, but she died of cancer when I was three and I don't have any memories of her at all.

"See, kiddo," Dad continues, "There are things about this I don't think you understand. This whole thing with your mom is complicated and I didn't want to burden you with our marital issues and all the stuff that's in the past. I think that was wrong. I'm going to be very truthful with you about what's going on from here on out. You're a smart kid and I'm going to trust that you will get it. So, here's where I'm coming from. This master's thing, it's complicated because it's not wrong that your mom wants to do this thing for herself. It's not wrong that she chose to do it. But that doesn't mean it didn't hurt you and Jen. I know it did and still is hurting you."

"Because I can't believe she CHOSE to go to Iowa and not stay with us," I shout.

"For 18 months, bud."

"Still..."

"Do you understand what I'm saying, though? Your mother having this dream, this goal for herself, is not wrong even though it's hard on us. We've talked about this before, bud. Your mom didn't have the chance to get her master's when she was younger, like she'd planned. She got accepted into an excellent school in New York City and then we learned we were having you, which will always be the most awesome thing that ever happened to us. But she's dedicated all this time, 14 years, to you, me and Jen. She took care of your grandpa after Grandma died, too. She finally does something for herself and applies for her master's again and gets in. She actually gets in! I don't think you understand how difficult it is to get into Iowa for poetry. I really didn't get it at first, either."

I cross my arms and sit stone-faced. I hate it when he says I don't "get it," as if I'm some dumb kid who can't understand the ways of the world, or something.

"I do get it, Dad. I just don't agree with it. I don't think we ought to forgive her so easily. You always let her off the hook. Always."

He sighs, heavily and continues. "Did you know Iowa only takes 25 poetry students every year. 25, tops."

"Yes, you've told me that about a dozen times. And, when you talk about getting pregnant with me before Mom could go back to school, it makes me feel like this is all my fault. Like my being born made all of this happen."

"Oh no, that's not at all how I want you to feel. Come here," Dad says, holding his arm open. I look at him but stay put.

"Come over here, right now!"

I walk over and he wraps his arm around my shoulder, squeezing me a little.

"Honey, that's not what I'm saying. It's just... some couples who marry young can weather the storms and all the changes that come at them. You change so much in your twenties. Other couples struggle, and it looks like your mom and I are in that category."

"Mom is, anyways," I say. "It seems like you've always been happy."

Dad blinks. I can see he's thinking about his reply to that.

"I can be pretty oblivious. I'll be honest, I knew things were a little stressful, but I thought it was everything your mom was going through with your grandma, and the grief. I knew, deep down, something was off between us. But I ignored it. I think I was in denial because I didn't want anything to be wrong. I like structure and stability. I do not like a lot of change."

"That's how I am. I can't handle major changes."

"Well, that's not something I would have chosen to pass on to you. We'll both have to work on adapting, bud. Makes life a whole lot easier."

I nod and step away so I can look at him. "Do you think you and Mom will divorce? Do you still love her?"

"I sure hope not and, yes, I do love her. Absolutely. I don't like that she kept her plans from me for that little while, but even that is complicated."

I also really hate when grown-ups say something's complicated and stop at that. "What do you mean?"

Dad takes a swig of his coffee and makes a face. "This is cold. Let me get a fresh cup."

I grab his mug. "I'll get it." I go over to the sink, dump the cold stuff out and pour a fresh cup for him. Then, I put in a splash of cream. Dad's smiling when I sit it down in front of him.

"Thanks."

I give him a peace sign.

"To answer your question, when you get older, you start to see that you actually have very little time on earth. Very little time. If you're the kind of person who has something big you want to accomplish, like going back to school, you feel a lot of pressure. The older you get, the stronger that pressure gets. The decision you make may seem selfish but when you have a huge opportunity, like your mom does, to make your life-long dream come true, what do you do?"

"Well, if she realized she has so little time," I say, "you'd think she'd want to spend her time with me and Jen. Did she even think about how we'd feel, me and Jen?"

"Of course she did, kiddo. You didn't see how many times

she cried about leaving you kids." He puts his hand on my shoulder again and squeezes.

"Why doesn't she act like she misses us, then? I know she says she does, but she really doesn't act like it. She seems happy and excited about everything she's doing in Iowa."

Dad shakes his head. "I don't know, kiddo. Maybe she thinks being upbeat is what's best. Parents have to leave their kids for a variety of reasons. Think about parents who are in the military or who get transferred by their companies. They have to leave their families. It does happen."

"Mom had a choice."

"Iowa Writers' Workshop is one of the best schools in the nation for a master's of fine arts. She didn't even think she'd be accepted. She sent her application out as a sort of long shot. Then, she got accepted and it started to feel like she didn't have a choice. It really is a wonderful opportunity for her. Now that she's there, I see how she's growing. I wouldn't want her to miss out on that."

"You already explained all of that. You know it's worse for Jen," I say. "She's only ten. What about her?"

"Jen and your mom video chat almost every night, sometimes for over an hour. You could, too, if you were here more often, and willing. You know, your mom was so distracted the last couple of years. And she was grieving and depressed. I'd bet these chats are giving them more quality time than they've had since Jen was little. So don't worry, kiddo. Jen will be fine. We're all going to be fine." He stands and comes up next to me, wrapping his arm around my shoulder.

I take a deep breath. I know I'll never forget how much Jen cried the week Mom left. Sure, she seems better now but who knows the psychological damage that's already been done.

"I don't know…I don't think I can ever forgive her." With no warning at all, I start sobbing.

"Oh, bud, give it some time. Will you do that? And tell her what you're feeling. Please try."

I shrug.

"Come on," he says, jabbing me in the shoulder over and over. Finally, I nod.

"OK, I'll try. But Dad," I say quietly, "Promise you won't ever leave us. I don't think I could handle that."

He squeezes my shoulder again, bending to look me in the eyes. "What? Of course I won't. What do you think, I'm gonna run off with the circus again?"

We smile at each other a minute. Then he asks, "Hey, learned a new one. Why did the bear refuse the magician's offer to make him human?"

I roll my eyes. "I don't know. Why?"

"Being someone else would've been *unbearable*."

He grins and winks at me. I groan, loudly.

* * *

THAT NIGHT, I talked to my mom for a few minutes on Zoom, mostly to make Dad happy. She talked about Grandpa and how bad she felt. She cried a little. I think Dad must have talked to her about not being all happy-phony, or whatever. It didn't quite feel like "us," but it was more normal, in a way. I could tell Mom was anxious and excited to come home for Thanksgiving. She told me she couldn't wait, like, five times.

23
PRESTO CHANGE-O

Today, we went to church and performed a short show for the Sunday School classes. We do a trick for church groups where we turn water into wine, so to speak. That always goes over well.

We took Grandpa to the Heidelberg, his favorite German restaurant. His surgery is tomorrow, and I want to be there for my grandpa and Dad, but I still haven't heard from Gini. I'm desperate to talk to her. And tomorrow is the start of basketball tryouts.

I nearly had a panic attack on the drive home from church, thinking about all that's happening tomorrow. I played the music Gini sent for meditating and it did help. I'll admit, I even cried a little. It's weird, but crying sometimes helps me feel better, for whatever reason.

* * *

AFTER DINNER, I meet up with Lamar, Sal, and Drake at the basketball courts for one last practice. They spend an hour taking me through the drills and some of the basic stuff they had to do at last year's tryout: blocking, passing, shooting, layups. I've gotten way better since spring. Plus, my arms are a little muscular for the first time, and I almost have a two-pack. I think Mom is going to be surprised. I bet I'm taller than her now, too.

While we play, Sal mentions a new girl who's moved in next door to him. He doesn't know her name but, apparently, she's from Seattle and is good at poi.

"What the heck is poi?" Drake asks.

"It's this thing that started in Hawaii. You ever seen the balls of fire they swing around?" Drake laughed. "You ever seen balls on fire, man?" We all cracked up at that one.

"You guys want to come over to watch her do her poi ball routine? She doesn't use fire, but she's got some that glow in the dark and I can see her out my bedroom window, practicing. She's out there every night. Seriously, check this out." Sal pulls up a photo he's taken of her.

"That's cool!" Drake exclaims. "Sure, I'll come over."

"I better get home," I tell the crew, tossing the ball to Lamar.

"I have an algebra test tomorrow," Lamar tells them. "I need to get home and study."

* * *

ON MY WALK HOME, I check my phone for the millionth time that day. Still no word from Gini. Dad is sitting on the couch, watching the most boring history show on earth.

"How's it going?" Dad asks.

I take a deep breath, walk over to the couch, and lean over the back, next to him. I can smell his aftershave he's worn my whole life. For some reason, that smell always makes me feel happier. Dad reaches his hand back and tousles my hair.

"Hey!" I say, sweeping it back into place. Dad chuckles a bit.

On the walk back from the b-ball courts, I'd decided I was

going to offer to go with my dad to the hospital. It's the right thing to do, even if it meant missing the first day of tryouts. Before I can say anything, he tells me Jen is going home with a new friend, Valerie, and that he'll pick us both up around six p.m. tomorrow – her from Valerie's and me from the house.

"Are you sure you don't want me to go to UM with you and Grandpa?" I ask, even though I. Am. So. Relieved.

"Heavens no, you don't need to be there for the surgery," he says.

Thinking about what they're going to do to my grandpa tomorrow makes me feel ill. I'm dreading seeing him after the surgery. It's going to be a tough week. If Gini breaks up with me now, I don't know what I'm going to do.

24
BLIND SHUFFLER

Dad said he could drive us to school on his way to get Grandpa for his surgery, which starts at 10. I'm a little early, so I throw my stuff in my locker and go wait by Gini's locker. My heart is pounding a million miles a minute, watching for her to walk down the hallway. The halls are filling up and I peer through the crowd, but don't see her. I don't know if her bus is late or what, but it seems like it's taking forever.

Then the halls start emptying out and, right as I'm about to head to first hour, I spy her walking toward me. She's walking alone, looking super depressed.

"Gini," I call to her, raising my hand in a wave, as if she can't see me in a totally empty hall. *What a dork!* I think. She stops dead in her tracks when she looks up. No smile. My heart sinks.

"Are you OK? What happened?" I quiz her when she gets closer. "I've been worried sick!"

The bell rings and her face scrunches up. I know Gini hates walking in late, having everyone stare at her. She turns to open her locker and says, "Can we talk about this during lunch? We're really late."

GUT PUNCH. It feels like my heart literally drops to my stomach. I feel butterflies and NOT the good kind.

"I kind of have to know, Gini. I can't go to class like this. Look at me." I show her my hand, which is literally shaking. "I've been waiting all weekend. You couldn't call me, not even once?"

I know it sounds like I'm accusing her when I'm the one who should be apologizing. I start to say how sorry I am when she cuts me off.

"My parents told me I have to stop seeing you," Gini blurts out.

"Are you kidding?"

"No matter what I say. I told them we're really good friends and that you had wanted to show me around for my birthday, which they canceled."

"They canceled your sleepover? Oh my God. I'm sorry, Gini!"

"It doesn't matter. It wouldn't have been fun anyway. So that's basically it and I don't know what to do now." She scowls again and tries to shove all her books into the locker at once. They fall with a bang to the floor.

"Here, let me help, k?" I say. "You're right. We should get to class. I'll find you at lunch. Let's go get our passes together and head to class. I'm sure we can think of something."

I help her put her books away and slam the locker closed. Gini looks at me sideways, like she's trying to figure something very important out.

"What is it?" I ask.

Mr. Morris sticks his head out of the science lab. "Kids, come on," he says. "What are you doing out here?"

"Sorry Mr. Morris," I tell him. "We'll get our passes and head to class."

We walk down the hallway, past the library and the courtyard. It feels like there's this barrier between us now, like those weird, invisible dog fences. Gini is normally so talkative but she's completely quiet. She also is the one who usually takes my hand. I notice she has both arms tightly wrapped around her books. Now I'm really starting to worry. I think she IS going to break up with me.

Mrs. Rudolph stares at us from behind her computer. She fills out our passes to get into class and then, grumpily, she says, "Here you go, lovebirds." I swear, the school staff can be so immature sometimes.

I drop Gini off to her Spanish class and head to math. I want to kiss her so bad, but she rushes through the door before I can even ask. I want everything to be back to how it was only three days ago, before I talked her into totally betraying her parents and blew it all to smithereens.

Lamar is in my math class, and I see him mouth, "What's up?" when I walk by his desk. I quickly write a note and sneak it to him:

Not good, dude

I have to get through math, English and social studies before lunch – literally THE longest classes in the history of my middle school career.

When the bell rings, I bolt to the lunchroom. Then I stand at the door, watching for Gini. People keep treating me like I'm some greeter. They keep high fiving me, saying, "Yo!" and stuff like that. I try to ignore them. Finally, I see Gini walking with Sophie, who gives me a sad wave. I can see the pity in Sophie's eyes as she walks away, leaving us.

"Want to go to the courtyard for a minute?" Gini asks. I nod and we walk straight to the door to the courtyard to claim a spot at the back picnic table. I say a silent prayer that no one will come and bug us. I say a second one that this is not the end for me and Gini.

Gini tells me that she's grounded for a month – no friends, phone, or even television. That was after a full inquisition and a whole bunch of yelling. Her mom even cried, Gini says. She was upset by Gini lying, mostly.

I feel so incredibly guilty. My dad doesn't even know about our date. I doubt I'd be in trouble even if he did find out. I've never had strict parents, so it's a little hard for me to imagine what that's like. I don't know what to do or say. I keep saying "sorry" over and over, like a dummy.

"You don't have to keep saying you're sorry. I'm not mad at you," Gini tells me. "But I don't know what to do. If my parents find out we're still dating, or whatever, I'll be grounded forever and will lose all of their trust."

I nod. "I guess that means we have to break up, then." I feel a little sick to my stomach when I blurt that out, but I'd rather be the one to say it first. Gini takes a deep breath. *Please let her disagree. Please!*

"My parents are probably way different from what you're used to. How could you know that, though? Did you know their marriage was arranged? They didn't get to pick each other. They only met one time before their wedding. That's how they do it, mostly, in India."

I know I looked confused. *Why is she telling me this right now?*

"Is that what they want you to do?" I ask. I can't imagine not knowing who you're going to marry and spend the rest of your life with. Marriage seems complicated enough as it is.

"My mother has talked to me about it, a little bit. I'm not sure what they're thinking but I know what I want. I'm going to pick who I want to be with, you know?"

I nod. The sadness in her eyes is scaring me.

"But, right now, I can't stand having my parents angry at me, doubting me all the time, not if I want to earn their trust again. I think we do have to break up. I'm so sorry." Her face is turning bright red and I can see tears in her eyes. She's blinking really fast to try not to cry.

I scooch in closer and put my arm around her shoulder.

Students start to fill up the yard and all the tables, crowding onto ours, jostling and laughing. Some jokester yells, "Get a room!" to us. I stare at Gini, but what I really feel like doing is getting up from the picnic table, walking straight over to the smart-alec jerk and punching him in the mouth. I close my eyes for a few seconds. This isn't at all what I was expecting, I realize. I somehow thought it would work out with Gini.

She's breaking up with me. She's actually doing it. Maybe it's the sun beating down, but I start to feel a little sick to my stomach. I thought she'd be in trouble, but this is WAY worse, and I don't know how to fix it. I don't think I can fix it.

Gini wipes away a single tear that's running down her cheek. That's when I think about her gift. I've been carrying it around in my backpack all this time.

"It's OK, Gini, I get it," I whisper, practically into her hair. Then I lean over and dig around in my backpack. I don't even care if people see. I want to try to cheer her up. I pull the gift out and have a split-second hope that maybe she'll change her mind when she sees it, and we can stay together in secret. This might be my one and only chance.

"So, I was going to give this to you Friday, but then with your parents and everything, I lost track of time..." I hand her the plaque. Her eyes grow wide, and she smiles for the first time all day.

"What?! Oh my gosh, that is so nice," she gushes.

"I'm sorry it's not wrapped."

Gini stares at it. "Did you make this?" she asks, turning it over. I etched, "Love, Jay" onto the back.

"My grandpa helped but, mostly, yeah, I made it for you. Do you like it?"

"It's beautiful. I love it," she says. Then, she gives me a huge hug. I'm so surprised I barely hug her back. "I said get a room!" the jerk yells again. I flip him the finger, and Gini and I both start laughing. The way she looks at me gives me a little hope that she's changing her mind, until she asks, "Can we stay friends?"

No, not friends, I want to scream. Instead, I give her a thumbs up.

"Well, I guess that's it, then," she says, standing. I stand up, too, and we look at each other, awkwardly. Then, she starts to walk toward the cafeteria, and I follow her in.

"Hey, can you tell your grandpa I said thanks for this?" Gini asks.

I say, "Sure."

My grandpa! I forgot about what's happening until right then. He's probably in surgery at this very moment. *Ugh, I feel so selfish again.*

Gini gives me a quick wave before she walks over to her table. I don't feel like eating, so I walk straight out to the hallway. I go sit in the office (after asking Mrs. Rudolph if it's OK) and text my dad to see how everything is going. I'm relieved when Dad tells me Grandpa is out of surgery and it went fine.

> He wants us to call him Stumpy! Still trying to make us laugh. He's amazing! I'll see you and Jen around 6. K?

> Ok

How much worse can this day be? I think.

25
SQUEEZE BOX

At the hospital, I take Jen's hand as we walk in. It smells like disinfectant the minute we walk up to the front desk. Dad picks up a bottle of hand sanitizer and squirts some in each of our palms. A nice lady gives Jen a coloring book and a box of colored pencils and then we head to the elevator.

"Do we have to look at it?" Jen asks my dad as we walk down the long corridor, past the gift shop.

"Grandpa's leg, you mean?" Dad looks down at her and then over at me. "Of course not, honey. It'll be covered with a blanket."

I must have sighed louder than I meant to because he reaches over and tousles my hair.

"It's ok, bud. Both of you. It's going to be all right. Your grandpa's a trooper. He survived Vietnam; he can survive this. He's already joking around. You know how he is. I told you how he wants us to call him Stumpy, didn't I?"

I nod. We pass the cafeteria and Jen asks if we can eat dinner there. It doesn't smell too bad, actually. Dad says sure and tells us we won't be staying long. *Hopefully, our visit will make*

Grandpa happy, I think, as we ride up the elevator to the seventh floor.

It is weird to see him lying in the hospital bed. He's sleeping when we get to his room and he looks shrunken, somehow. I can't help but look at where his leg used to be. Dad gently touches his shoulder and Grandpa slowly opens his eyes.

"Dad, I've brought Jay and Jenna to see you."

Grandpa kind of sputters for a second. His eyes are a little crusty. I've never seen him look this frail and it scares me. *Can people die from losing a leg?* I wonder.

"Well, hello there, kiddos!" He's trying hard to sound chipper, even though his voice is scratchy. I know it's for our benefit. He opens his arms and both Jen and I rush over to hug him, me on one side of his hospital bed and Jen on the other.

"Now that's a hug sandwich if I ever had one!" he says, laughing. Jen starts whimpering a little. "Don't worry, don't worry, your ol' Grandpa is fine. In fact, I'm going to be better than new before you know it! They're going to give me a bionic leg to replace my old one. Did you know that? What do you think of them beans, huh?"

Jen giggles a little. She keeps staring at the place where his leg should be. "Jen, stop staring like that!" I tell her.

"It's fine," Grandpa says.

The nurse comes in, then, says hi and reaches to pull the sheet back when Dad stops her. "Let me take the kids out before you do that," he says. "Dad, we'll go get a little something to eat and will be back soon."

"No," I say, surprising myself. "I want to stay."

Dad and Grandpa exchange a look.

"I'll be fine," I insist. "I want to stay with Grandpa."

They are all silent for a minute. The nurse looks at us, waiting patiently.

"Fine," Dad finally says. I'm relieved when they leave. Grandpa always has a way of making me feel like everything will be all right. Even then, while the nurse is getting ready to check his bandages, I feel calmer than I've felt all day.

"You don't have to look." Grandpa winks at me.

"I'm OK," I say, though I do try to keep my eyes on Grandpa's face.

"You know I nearly lost that darn leg in the Vietnam War? That's a story for another day. I've been dying to know, how'd that gal, Gini, like the gift you made her?"

That's when I lose it. Flat out, 100%, start bawling like a baby. The nurse stops and stares at me, her eyes bugging out.

"It's OK, it's all right," Grandpa says.

"I'm almost done," the nurse explains, motioning to the IV.

"Oh no, Becky, it'll be fine. Go on ahead and finish up whatever you have to do," he says, pulling me toward him. I lay on his chest, crying harder than I can ever remember. I don't even care that the nurse is there and don't notice when she leaves. Finally, I lift my face up.

"Now," Grandpa says. "What's all this about?"

I shake my head. "I don't need to talk about it… just been a really bad day but I don't want to burden you. You've been through enough. It's nothing."

"Nonsense," Grandpa says. "Sit up and tell me, or I'll worry about all sorts of things." I tell him about Gini and then add, "I guess I miss Mom, too." I start crying again. It's like a dam burst and I can't stop the stupid tears from flowing out of my gosh darn eyes. Here Grandpa is with his leg gone and I'm blubbering to him about my little problems, like an idiot.

"Well, of course you miss her, sweetie. If I'd ever known it would have this kind of impact on you and Jen, I never would have insisted she go. She came to me for advice, and I told her she should do it. When you have a kid, no matter what age they are, you want all their dreams to come true. Such a huge opportunity to live her dream. I thought you would be fine. I mean, it's only 18 months. I know now how long that must seem to you and Jen. I wasn't thinking about that when I told her to go, and I'm sorry about that."

I don't know what to say. I nodded and tried to think through what he was telling me. Grandpa told her to go?

"Why?"

"Why'd I tell her to go?"

I nodded.

"Have you ever read any of your mother's poetry?"

I shake my head no. *I'd never even thought to ask to read it.*

Grandpa nods his head, slowly. "You should. Then, you'd see why I encouraged her. She's talented, that mother of yours. She has something very special. It's hard to explain. And I could see she was struggling, depressed after your grandma died. I thought, what's 18 months? Her eyes lit up when she talked about it, and how she could get a teaching job after that and, hopefully, start publishing more of her work."

Grandpa was starting to sound tired, his voice growing softer as he spoke. "She'll be back in three weeks or so, for Thanksgiving. You ought to read some of what she's been working on the past few weeks. She's been sending me some stuff through email. I can't believe how much she's grown with her poetry, already. I'm so proud of her and I hope you can be, too."

26
WHO IS THIS HOUDINI GUY?

Before school, I lie and tell Dad I've got to stay after the next few days for Robotics Club so I can't pick Jen up. Luckily, he's taken off the next two days to get the house around for Grandpa to come stay with us while he recuperates. At least, I'm catching a break on that one!

First thing, when I get home from the second day of tryouts, Dad is standing at the dining room table surrounded by Amazon boxes.

"Oh good, you're home," he says. "I have a surprise for the talent show. Come check these out!" He does a spin and I see he's wearing a new black jacket. It looks purposefully old-fashioned. He holds up another, matching one that looks like it's about my size.

Oh NO! I think. *He went and bought new magic outfits!*

"Look at this cool tailcoat!" he's genuinely gushing. "It's vintage steampunk. Kids love steampunk! Gold stitching, shoulder chains...the works!"

"Dad, kids don't like steampunk," I blurt out. "How much did you pay for these?" *I really hope it wasn't much and that they can be returned.*

"They were only $150 apiece. I thought we could put a gold, sparkly rim around our top hats. Maybe get away from the red cape, even. I've come to think it's time for change. Here, try it on."

I step back like he's handing me a venomous snake. Dad looks confused and a little angry.

"Can you get your money back?" I ask.

He's looking at the jacket and then back at me. "I thought you'd really dig these. You're always complaining about our outfits. Complaining about a lot of things, to tell you the truth. I thought you wanted a change."

"YES, Dad, I DO want a change but I kind of want a say in the change. I have my own ideas. You never let me make any of the decisions about our show. I'm SO sick of it!!!"

I head toward his door, getting ready to storm out.

"Ok, fine. What would you wear, if you could choose?" He sounds a little snarky, but I stop at the door and turn. I don't even have to think about it.

"Black t-shirt and a pair of jeans. Tight-fitting jeans, not the baggy kind Mom keeps buying for me."

I can see Dad's head spinning. That is NOT his type of magic outfit. Dad stands there for a minute, his hands on his hips, looking at me sideways.

"So, OK, let me think about this out loud. You want to wear something more casual, or 'cas' as you young folks say it?"

I try hard not to roll my eyes. I'm happy he's even listening to my idea, not that he'll really let me choose.

"Yup, that's what I would wear."

"So... no logo, I suppose?"

"Nope."

"No top hat? You gotta have a top hat."

"Nope. And no cape, either."

Dad pauses a minute, then looks overly horrified. He pretends to stab himself in the chest and falls back onto the couch, making it squeak under his weight. Then, he sits up and stares at me for a good, long time. I know he's making fun. Any minute now, he'll say "No way, José!" or something equally cringy.

"OK," he says, nodding.

"What?"

"All right, we can do that."

"Really?" I ask. Now I'm the one shocked. I don't know what to say. We stare at each other for a few seconds.

"Yes, it's high time for a change but I would look utterly ridiculous in tight jeans. You wear what you said, and I'll wear my kind of jeans with a black button-down dress shirt. I've seen a lot of the newer magicians doing that. We'd match and..." he stops for a minute, gets this faraway look on his face. I don't know if he's serious or purposefully being overly dramatic to try to make me laugh.

"You know," he says, turning his head toward me, slow-motion, "I think we'll be looking rather like a snack!"

Um, no. "Dad, have you been looking stuff up on Urban Dictionary again? Because N period O period."

He's grinning. Then, he holds his hand up like I'm supposed to give him a high five. I laugh but do walk over and give him a high five. Can't leave him hanging there, all pitiful.

"So," Dad says, "What else?"

"What else, what?"

"What else would you change about the show? I know you watch Shin Lim, Mike Hammer, and all those new guys out there. Is there something we could do to spruce up our act for the talent show? Make it more relevant and hipper?"

There's nothing I can think of that will save us from the humiliation of that talent show.

That's what I want to say, but I stall. I take a few deep breaths. "I really don't know, Dad," I tell him, honestly.

"Come on, Jay! I'm asking for your input. What are your thoughts about the middle school talent show?"

I stare at him and feel my hands getting sweaty. My heart is racing. I know it's time to come clean about everything, but it's so hard when he's looking at me all smiley and happy. Makes me tear up a little, to be honest. Still, I have to tell him, no matter what happens.

I take one more deep breath and say, "Dad, I don't know if doing the talent show is the best idea. I have to be honest. I'm really nervous about it."

I can feel a lump in my throat. I'm so stressed, but I did it! I told him what I'd been thinking for weeks. It feels good to get it off my chest, but scary. I brace myself for the backlash.

"Hmm, I see," he says. "Well, think about it and get back with me. If we're going to do the show, we have about three weeks to get some new tricks down. As far as that goes, we could stick with all new tricks and do a much shorter show, like 10 minutes or so. Think about it, bud, OK? You have a real talent. I know I don't tell you this often, but you are WAY better than I was at your age. You really could go someplace with your magic, even if it's side gigs to pay your way through college. I mean, would you rather sling beers at some seedy bar, like I did, or do magic shows? Food for thought."

Dad reaches over to me and puts his arms out for a hug. I lean in and hug him back. I can't believe he's taking it this good. It makes me feel stupid for not telling him sooner. It honestly feels amazing to have that off my chest, like a weight has lifted.

"I'm happy you told me, Jay. I knew something was off but couldn't put my finger on it. Look, this is *your* middle school talent show. If we're going to do a show together, or you want to do one by yourself, I want it to be one you're proud of. I want it to be something that comes from your heart, you know?"

I nod, still in shock. Dad starts to get up and walks toward the kitchen island.

"Dad?" I stop him before he walks away.

"Yeah, bud," he says, looking down at me.

"There's something else I've been meaning to ask."

He walks back over to the couch and sits next to me. "Shoot," he says.

"I tried out for basketball. Can I play this season if I make the team?"

"What? When did you do that?" he asks. He acts as if it's the most shocking thing he's ever heard.

"Tryouts started Monday," I say it, weakly.

"What do you mean? Like, yesterday? Is that why you stayed after?"

"Yeah, today was the second day of tryouts."

"What about Robotics Club?"

My face is turning bright red. I feel like such a jerk for lying to him the way I did.

"I'm sorry I lied. I'm not in Robotics Club anymore. I only joined because I liked that girl, Gini. Then, yesterday, she broke up with me." It's surprising how fast you can go from feeling great about things, like I was a minute ago, to super low.

"I see," is all dad says. "I see," he says, again, sitting back down on the couch. He has this weird, far-away look on his face. I wish he'd scream at me, or something.

"I don't understand, bud. Why didn't you tell me you had tryouts? Or about this Gini girl? I didn't even know you were going together. This is the first I've heard that. Have I been that out of sorts that you felt like you couldn't tell me these things?"

I can't say anything. My face feels like it's burning and I'm trying hard not to cry. I'm SO sick of crying.

"Look, it's OK, bud."

I hang my head, can't even look at him. I'm so ashamed. First, I have all these terrible thoughts about my dad and how lame I think the shows are now. I lied to him and kept secrets. I was so worried about disappointing him, I didn't even give him a chance.

And now I know I was wrong for doing that. This is the same exact thing Mom did to him, and now I did it, too. She didn't want to disappoint him, so she kept her big secret until the last minute. I've been so judgmental of her and I'm just as bad, if not worse! We were both very wrong to do that to my dad.

"I'm sorry I didn't tell you earlier, Dad. I didn't want to be another disappointment to you," I confessed. "But you didn't deserve this." And I start gosh-darn crying again.

"Look at me, son," Dad tells me. "You are anything but a disappointment. I'm so proud of you, I can hardly contain it. It's been a hard few months and you've really stepped up to be there for me, to help out with Jen and even your grandpa. I haven't been myself, either. We all make mistakes and, you know, families forgive each other. At least, this one does."

"You'll forgive me?"

Dad smiles, and I can see he's a bit teary, too. "Of course, I forgive you. You're my main man. My buddy. My partner. There's nothing you could ever do to make me stop loving you. You're stuck with me – all of you – including your mom and Jen!"

I scoot over toward him on the couch and lean my head on his shoulder. We sit there for a few seconds. I can't remember the last time I felt peace like this.

I lift my head and tell him, "I really hope I can be like you, Dad, someday."

My dad smiles down at me. "Well, you know what they say?" he asks.

"Flattery will get you everywhere!" we say in unison and start laughing. I feel light and happy.

"When will you find out if you made the team?"

"Friday."

Dad nods.

"Well, actually, I think it's great you're going out for basketball. What's that look for? I totally support you going out for a sport. I never knew you had an interest, that's all. I mean, outside of knocking the ball around with your crew. If that's what you want to do, go for it. Why would you not tell me? Why would you think you'd have to lie about that?"

"Because it'll mean I'd have to skip out on some of the shows," I say. "And I wouldn't be around to practice as much."

Dad is silent for a few seconds, and I can tell he's deep in thought. He takes a couple of drinks of his water.

"You know, bud, it's probably time for me to create a solo show. I mean, you'll be going off to college in less than five years. That seems crazy to say! But we're not always going to be able to perform together. Jen has never shown a particular interest, I don't think."

"She's into fashion. Did you know she's been vlogging?"

"What? For crying out loud, has my head been up in a cloud that much lately?"

I can't believe he's the one feeling bad. I've been deceptive and secretive. Leave it to my dad to blame himself.

"It's not your fault, Dad. I should have told you about all that stuff. I'm really sorry."

"No, don't be. I've been stubborn. That's one of the things I'm learning about myself in therapy."

I stare at him. He's been keeping secrets, too.

"I didn't know you were going to therapy. Is Mom going, too?"

"Yes, we're doing Zoom therapy together. I think it's really helping. We're hoping to have some family sessions with you and Jen, too. It's nice to have someone to sort your problems out with."

"Sure, that'd be cool," I say. I'm genuinely glad he and mom have been getting therapy, and that it's helping.

"Jay, I'd love it if we could still do the shows when you're able to, but not at the expense of you exploring your own sports and hobbies. I should have made that clearer to you." He looks at me straight in my eyes, in a way he hasn't in ages.

All that time I was so worried and plotting and all I had to do was be honest about stuff. If I were a cartoon character, my jaw would be hanging to the floor!

"OK?" he asks.

I nod. "Thanks, Dad," I tell him.

"For what?"

"For taking me seriously. And for telling me about the counseling. For being a great dad."

He nods and smiles, turning his head away. I can see he's starting to choke up again.

Maybe a shorter, cooler show wouldn't be so bad, I think. I'll have to run it by the crew.

* * *

ALL THE TIME I spent practicing for tryouts seemed to pay off. I was surprised to be able to keep up with the team, for the most part. I even sunk a three-pointer on the last day. Lamar shouted, "Way to go!" and the coach even slapped me on the back. Trying out with my dad's support was the best part of all.

After tryouts, while Sal, Lamar, and I are walking home, I tell them about the convo with my dad. I run the idea of the shorter, new show by them, and they both think it might go over OK at the talent show. Something short and sweet was how I put it.

"Your dad's not wrong, you know?" Lamar says. "I never thought you quitting magic altogether was a good idea. I didn't want to say anything, but you'd be throwing away a lot of years of practicing. It would be like me giving up on animation."

"Yeah," adds Sal. "You've always had a knack for magic."

MIDDLE SCHOOL IS NO PLACE FOR MAGIC

* * *

AFTER THEY PEEL OFF, a lot of the things I like about magic start flooding back to me. I always liked the idea of being part of a special society. Dad has introduced me to lots of magicians from all over the country. There's a whole magic community most people don't even know exists. It's cool that only one person out of, like, 25,000 even knows how to perform magic tricks. Plus, magicians are notoriously crazy. They are always trying things that are way over the top. Heck, some even die trying their illusions. But some really are insanely amazing, like Blackthorn swallowing a jackhammer, Blaine spitting up live frogs (GROSS) and, of course, the old Penn and Teller bullet catch.

For the first time in what seems like months, I'm happy to be walking through our door. I tell Dad right away that I want to rework the routine for the talent show and Dad slaps his hands together. I give him a short run-down of the tricks I'd like to try.

"Ok, well, this is exciting! I think you might be onto something, kiddo. Go tell your grandpa, why don't you? I brought him home this morning and he's staying in Jen's room with her. She insisted. What are you thinking, like, glow-in-the-dark balloons for the finale with Mabel? That would be easy enough to switch out. I'll see what Ray at Fab Magic can put together for us." Dad gets chatty when he's worked up.

"Sure, that would be cool," I tell him. "Plus, I saw Ray has this LED baton at the store. You can draw things with it, like poi, and I thought we could incorporate the school song and, like, maybe I could draw the mascot. Just a simple version of an Eagle. Something like that. And maybe color-changing hoops?" *Something that'll impress Gini,* I think. Dad is beaming. For the first time in forever, I start to get excited about magic.

27
"ALL THE MAGIC I HAVE KNOWN I'VE HAD TO MAKE MYSELF"

My nerves are shot. I made the basketball team. (YES!) Now, I have to get prepared to play in front of people. I don't know why I never thought of that before. Gini and her friends are probably all going to be there, staring down at us. Being on the court feels a lot like being a hapless fish in a bowl. I pray I don't flop! I'm really going to have to put those meditation tricks to good use the next two weeks leading up to our first game. I do think it'll be OK, once I get the hang of things, though. When I first started doing magic shows, I'd get super nervous. I don't even sweat doing our regular gigs anymore. It comes natural now. That's what I'm shooting for with basketball. It all comes down to practice. Lamar and I have been spending a lot of time at the court.

I've also been practicing for the talent show with Dad every chance we can get. Of course, I'm nervous about that, but the more we practice, the more excited I am to show off our new tricks. They are cool, if I do say so myself!

Thank goodness, b-ball practice was cut short today so Dad,

Lamar, and I can go through a dress rehearsal. The show's only 20 hours away and counting!

* * *

THE MOST CONFUSING thing is that I'm feeling more anxious about my mom coming home than playing basketball, the show, and everything else.

It's a weird feeling, being nervous about seeing your own mother. I wonder if I'll feel the same way about her. Will our hugs be awkward? Will we even have much to say to each other? I'm going to find out very soon.

Dad left at 5 o'clock to pick Mom up at the airport. I stayed back to finish making dinner. Jen and Grandpa are working on a puzzle together at the dining room table. They've had the puzzle pieces scattered all over for three days now. It's kind of a pain, but I look over at Grandpa and all I can think is how amazing he's doing. I bet my mom is going to be surprised. He does this thing now where he can scoot himself around in his wheelchair using one leg. Yesterday, he was fitted with his prosthetic. Dad took the day off to go with him and says he's going to be pretty sore until he gets used to it, but he should be walking again in a few months. I can tell Grandpa is relieved to have the surgery and fitting appointment behind him. He seems pretty much back to his normal self.

"Doesn't your sister look nice?" Grandpa asks, placing a piece of a kitten ear into the puzzle. His glasses are sliding way down his nose.

"Thanks Grandpa!" Jen says. She's taken to curling the front part of her hair but can't get to the back, which is oddly straight, and to wearing some makeup, too. I'm not sure Mom is going to be very happy about that. I think Jen looks silly in blush and lip gloss.

"You look good, Jen," I fib, stirring up the meat and adding in the taco seasoning.

"Do you need help, kiddo?" Grandpa asks. "I can quit working on the puzzle and chop the lettuce."

Right then, the car pulls up the driveway and stops next to the house. I turn the heat way down and go over to the kitchen door to look out. Both of my parents are getting out of the car, and they are both smiling. I notice that right away. My mom turns to look up at the house and sees me. Her eyes get that worried look and I dart back into the kitchen, out of sight. For a minute, I feel like running to my bedroom and locking my door. I have a bad feeling I'll say something and ruin Mom's homecoming for everyone.

The door creaks open, and she peeks her head in. "Hello, I'm home!" she says, quietly. Jen squeals and practically tackles her. Dad walks in behind and is beaming.

Looks like the car ride went well, I think.

I wish I didn't have this simmering feeling of resentment; that I could just run into her arms and be happy about her being home. But I stand in the kitchen, watching, until she's done being tackled by Jen. She walks toward me and hugs me, whispering, "I missed you, Jay." There's something about the way she smells, like the hand lotion she's always used, that makes me feel like I'm home for the first time since she left.

I cling to her for a few seconds, surprising both of us. Then, she held me back by my shoulders and says, "Wow, have you gotten taller. And look at those muscles. My handsome Jay!" She gushes. It's good to hear her voice.

After that, she turns and walks up to Grandpa. And she loses it. Totally. And I wasn't expecting that. Grandpa, sitting one-legged in his wheelchair and Mom practically crumbles into his lap, sobbing.

"I'm so sorry I wasn't there for you," she says. I didn't realize until right then how bad my mom felt about Grandpa. She pulls herself together pretty quickly but seeing her like that helps melt some of that simmering feeling I've been having for so long. At least, long enough that we are all able to sit and have a normal-feeling dinner.

* * *

"You can stay as long as you like," Dad tells Grandpa, cutting into the dessert (chocolate pie with whipped cream – Mom's fav).

"Ah, no, I'm anxious to get home. I'm getting around pretty well, and with you turning the library into my new bedroom, I can keep to the ground floor. Maybe Jen and Jay can come over to help with the laundry. That's really all I need."

"You did that?" Mom asks, looking at my dad, who nods and smiles.

"Yeah, we even had a hospital bed brought in and I put up some bars and a special toilet seat in the downstairs bathroom. I wanted to surprise you. I thought we'd all drive over to take a look at it later, if you're up for it, or we can go tomorrow, after the talent show. Whatever you want. I know you're probably tired after your flight and everything."

Mom stares at him, even reaches her hand out to pat my dad's. "I'm very grateful," she says, picking up dishes to takes them to the sink. I watch her squeeze Dad's shoulder when she walks by and see him smile up at her, the way he used to when they were happier.

"Either day, that sounds great," she says.

"Also, Dad's still getting a home nurse a couple times a week to help with showers and to check on his leg."

Mom puts the dishes in the sink. "That is wonderful. I'm so thankful for you, Jimmy. I really am." Her voice cracks a bit. She turns around to start rinsing the dishes in the sink, but I see her wiping tears on her shirt sleeve a couple times.

* * *

Mom knocks on my door around 8 p.m. I have our new magic show music on and am lying on my bed, going through the motions of our routine in my mind. Dad managed to talk Principal Evans into letting us use the projector and all the lights and equipment we needed for our dress rehearsal earlier in the day. It went off without a hitch, almost exactly like I'd seen it play out in my head.

"Come in," I say, a little too loudly. I click off the music. It's hard to stay angry with my mom. I do feel upset with her still, though. Less upset than earlier in the school year, but still…

Mom creaks the door open and peeks her head in.

"You have a minute?" she asks. Her oh-so-soft demeanor is a little irritating. That's not her normal voice. I wish she'd go back to her usual self, already.

"Yeah, of course," I say.

She walks over to the bed and sits down next to me.

"I've missed you so much, you know?" she starts.

I nod.

"Did you miss me?" she asks.

"Of course I did."

"It's so good to be home." She looks around the room. "I like the new poster." She points to my Glass Animals pineapple poster dad let me buy. "I have to say, I'm so impressed with you and your dad coming up with a new routine in, what, two or three weeks?"

"About three weeks but we mostly upgraded some of the tricks we've been doing for years. You'll see." *16 hours until curtain call!*

"I can't wait to see the show. I know you didn't want to do it, at first. What changed your mind?"

"I don't know. I guess, when Dad said I could redo everything, I got kind of excited. Then, Dad let the crew come over for a sleepover. We had pizza and everything. It was pretty dope. We did the show for them, and they all thought it was good. Having Lamar be a part of it is cool, too, combining our show with his animations. It's hard to explain. You'll see what I mean tomorrow."

"Lamar has a real gift with art. You do, too, hon. Daddy is so proud of you and so am I."

I nod. There is something I've been wanting to say to my mom for a few weeks now. I take a deep breath and exhale.

"I'm proud of you, too, Mom. I was mad at you for a long time, but I know it must be hard to be away from us, even if you're doing something you really like."

Mom sits very still for a few seconds. I can even hear the clicking of my alarm clock. Then, I see a tear trickle down her face and, for a second, I'm scared she is totally going break down again. Then, I'd break down and it'd be a *whole* thing. I'm relieved when she wipes the tear away and turns to me, smiling.

"Jay, that means the world to me!"

I nod, remembering what Grandpa said that night he was in the hospital. "You know, Mom? I've never even heard one of your poems. I really want to hear one."

"Really?"

I nod and say, "Yes, I really do."

Mom beams. "Well, OK, then. Hold tight." She takes off and is back in about a minute with one of her poetry books she'd been published in.

"So, this might help you see, well, kind of where I was when I applied to go to Iowa. Then, I want to read the one I wrote yesterday. Is that OK?"

"Yeah, of course."

I can tell she's a little nervous as she sits down next to me and opens the book to a page that's been marked. Then, she starts reading.

MIMI OLSON

The Dig
Let's take a look, again, at where we are

Examine the pieces of us
like an archaeological dig
Excavate our spats like
dinosaur bones
Dust them off,
put them on display,
the pros, the quid

Let's search for what went missing
to find some recognition
Among the broken shards
of our past

Or we could walk right on
by the site,
Let it go,
let it slide
Pretend
we have nothing to hide

IT'S SUPER QUIET, again. Mom is looking at me. Finally, I say, "I like it. It seems kind of sad, though." There are parts of it I'd have a read a few times to get it. Mostly, though, I figure it's about her and Dad.

"I was really struggling when I wrote that, kiddo."

"Yeah, it seems like you were lost, maybe? Is that what you were writing about?"

"That's a good read on this poem," she says. "That's exactly how I felt."

"What's the other poem you wrote?" I ask. "The one you finished this week?"

Mom takes out a notebook and opens it to the back.

"Whoa, did you fill all of that while you've been out there?" I ask her.

She nods. "It's been a pretty productive couple of months. This was the last one I wrote. It's still a simple draft. Keep that in mind." She reads.

Of All the Things

You forget the little things
That tie us together

The memories, a thousand, of us four
Emblems that fill my dreams

Remind me of the time I saw you
Through the kitchen window
Dancing to Prince with our baby girl

Oh, yes, I Would Die for You, too
How you cried the night my mother died
The play sword fights with our boy

I even miss the way you snore
I miss you, my love, to my core

"It's still very much a work in progress," Mom says and shuts the notebook. I look straight ahead for a few seconds. I watched her face while she was reading and it was very still, like now. I couldn't tell what she was thinking. I am glad she wrote this new one, a happier poem, about Dad.

"Have you showed this to him?" I ask.

Mom shakes her head. "I'm a little worried I've blown things. You, Jen and your dad are the best things in my life. You three are my life. I'm sorry it took me having to go away to realize what I have here. Adults don't always know what they want. And then, one day, it can strike you right out of the blue."

Her voice is shaking, again. I'm not sure I can speak, either, but I manage to squeak out, "You know Dad still loves you."

"I love him, too," Mom says, reaching over to pull me into a hug. "And I love you to pieces."

For the first time in months, I feel like the world is back in the right orbit. I feel like the sifting sand under my feet is solid ground again. I don't know any other way to explain it, the feeling that everything might work out, after all.

28
THIS MAGIC MOMENT

I enlisted Sophie and Morgan to get Gini in the front row. I even made sure to tape "reserved" signs on the three center seats so they'd know where she should sit for the talent show finale. Right before the show is about the start, I peek out to double check that Gini's sitting where I need her to be. They are nowhere in sight. In fact, the "reserved" seats are taken by three other girls.

"What the actual heck?" I say out loud. I text Sophie and Morgan.

> What gives?!?!

> Sorry 💀

> It's Sophie.

> What? Why?

> Bro, her parents are here cuz she's part of the Hindu dance thing

SO? I think. They could have saved the seat for her. Clearly, they do not understand the importance of Gini being in the front row.

> You have to get her in the front row! PLEASE!!!

> QUIT yelling at us!

> OMG, I'm not yelling.

Just then, I spot Gini on the other side of the stage, standing in a bright blue sari. She's surrounded by about a dozen other girls. It's a sea of colors.

Gini is facing me, but I can't tell if she sees me. Then, she waves toward where I'm standing. I look behind me and no one's there, so I turn back and wave at her. She motions down at her dress, shrugs and laughs. I remember when she told me she was sick of performing with the Hindu dance troupe. She must have given in to her parents, again.

Gini looks beautiful. Seriously, she could star in a Bollywood movie, but knowing she doesn't want to be in the dance makes me sad.

Gini points to me and gives a thumbs up. I *think* she's pointing at my new magician's outfit: jeans, black t-shirt, black tennis shoes. No cape, no top hat. Simple. Then I remember that I never got to tell her about the talk I had with my dad. She probably thinks I caved, too.

A friend taps her on the shoulder, and she turns away. I start to panic. Dad and I planned the entire routine around Gini being seated in that front row seat. Pacing, I stare at my phone to see if Sophie and Morgan were going to at least try to get her to the front row.

Nothing. No text from either of them. Looks like I'm out of luck.

I look in the front row and the three interlopers are still

there, guffawing it up. *Total hecklers, I can tell.* Sweat starts pouring out of my underarms. At least the t-shirt is black and will hide my pit stains.

"You OK?" Dad points at the phone, motioning for me to put it away and pointing to his watch. I know we only have a few seconds before the show starts. I nod at him right as the curtain goes up and Principal Evans walks to the mic to make the usual announcements and get the ball rolling.

I'm happy to see Gini's dance troupe is going first. She'll be able to watch the rest of the show! At least she'll see the finale I planned out for her. There are eleven talent acts total – some dancing, a couple of garage bands, a choral rendition of Taylor Swift songs. We're going last, right after the debate club's Hamilton-style political poetry rap.

By the time the debate club takes the stage, I'm so in my head, I don't hear a word of it. People are laughing and clapping loud, so it must have gone over OK.

At least they primed the audience for us, I think.

I take a deep breath, clenching and unclenching my fists, to pump myself up – part of my pre-show routine. I jump up and down a couple of times and shake my whole body out. I say a quick prayer and then, under my breath, I tell myself, *here we go. I'm ready. I've done these tricks over and over. I know the routine. I got this.*

I see Dad look me straight in my eyes. He gives me that slight nod. "Son," he says, smiling, and stepping back. I smile as I walk by him, and he winks.

I got this. I got this.

I walk onto the stage, my dad right behind me, and the music starts playing. I stand stage left and Dad is to my far right, in jeans and a black button-down shirt. The drums start up. Sal enlisted a few of his friends from band to play the school fight song for the first part of the act.

Dad and I start clapping for ten beats. The crowd joins in.

We had hoped that would happen, but I'm still a bit shocked it worked.

On the eleventh beat, we pull out our new LED laser batons and switch them on, playing it up a bit, like Han Solo. A few people in the audience laugh. I think one of them is my mom.

The lights go off and the stage lights are dimmed way down, like I'd instructed. The crowd gasps. I wasn't expecting that. *Might be a good sign.* Still on the same beat, we start drawing with the laser beams.

The cool thing about the new batons is how long the "drawings" last. Dad draws a tree and I draw an eagle, our school mascot, and they hang there, in the air, for several seconds.

We both click our lasers off right as Lamar clicks on the projector. He's set up at the back of the auditorium, manning this part of the show. The animated eagle he drew takes off, flapping across the black curtain behind us, and then flying against the wall. Again, I hear a definite gasp. The clapping stops and it's quiet except for the drums, still hammering out the school song. Then, Lamar's eagle balls itself up and dunks itself into the basket to our far right. It wasn't perfect, but it was still pretty cool looking. It was even better than in our dress rehearsal.

The audience erupts. They're clapping and cheering. Some of the basketball players start chanting, "Eagles! Eagles!"

I feel like pumping my fist in the air, but the lights are turning back on, washing over us. I wish I could see Lamar. I know he must be beaming. People are clapping to the beat again and everyone is chanting now.

Suddenly, a new worry pops in my head. *How in the world are we going to get everyone to calm down so we can keep going?* I look over at Dad, who's smiling. I can't tell if he's worried or not. He motions for the music to stop and the audience to quiet, putting his hands to his lips. They get it, somewhat, and start to tone it down.

While we're moving to our next spots, I scan the front row for my "mark" – the person I'll have to target for the finale instead of Gini. My eyes land on Gracy O'Dell, who I've known since, like, second grade. Gracy feels kind of like a cousin. Cousin-ish. OK, a distant cousin. It's perfect. *There's no way Gini would be jealous of Gracy*, I hope.

We have three tricks to get through before the finale. I focus in.

1. The first is our typical cup and ball routine, only with LED balloons and buckets. It took Dad and I a few days to switch over from our usual props. It goes off with only one small glitch that I don't think anyone even noticed. *Lots of claps. No heckling. So far, so good!*
2. We switched out our ring toss trick with color changing hoops. *They're clapping AND cheering at this point.*
3. Then, we do our levitation trick, only we incorporate the laser batons and, again, keep the lights dimmed. *Even more clapping.*

There is a little bit of a delay before the song, "Lay Your Head on Me," comes on. That's the song I chose for the finale. It's the last song Gini sent to me.

Meanwhile, Dad moves off stage left and I move to the center. I'm doing this part of the show solo.

The lights go down and I pull out the laser and turn it on. The crowd starts cheering. Then they start singing along with the song. I can't believe it. Everyone is having fun. My heart's practically pounding out of my chest.

I pull out a second beam. I get the red and the purple beams looping. I pull out a third and then a fourth and start juggling with them. *Crowd gasps.* I juggle for about ten more seconds, and then catch all the lasers. I take two lights in one hand and two lights in the other. Then, I draw a heart which beams out into the auditorium. I hope Gini knows that's for her.

I grab the bucket of glow-in-the-dark bracelets and toss them into the audience in handfuls. The crowd literally bursts into cheers. For a minute, I feel like I can't breathe. It's going better, *so much better,* than I ever imagined. One last set. One last set. *Please, please Lamar, let's get it right.*

I take the last laser prop out. It's a white laser. It turns on fine.

I draw a dove, just like we'd practiced, and watch the lines appear above everyone's head. I'd practiced this so many times, I could do it with my eyes closed. Then, on the exact right note of the song, I turn the laser off and Lamar's animated dove takes over. It flies, circling the auditorium once, before it starts descending to the chair I'd pointed at surreptitiously with my laser, marking Gracy so Lamar would know where to aim.

On the exact right beat, he shuts the animation off, and the lights turn on. I have to blink a few times to adjust to the light. *YES, LAMAR!! He did it!*

While Lamar's dove was circling, I'd snuck down to the front row. By the time the lights go on, I'm standing in front of Gracy. (I really wish it was Gini!) I'm already in the midst of folding an origami dove. Gracy is looking up at me, wide-eyed. I try not to look right into her eyes.

The next instant, right on the last note of the song, is the big reveal. From the audience's perspective, it looks like the origami dove has been turned into a real dove. Mr. Thompson, a magician friend of Dad's, let us borrow a real dove for the show. I let the dove fly away and he goes right to left stage, where Mr. Thompson is waiting. I really owe him!

The audience is cheering super loud now. Some people are standing. *Are they giving us a standing ovation?* I wonder. I quickly hand Gracy the origami dove which was meant for Gini. It only seems right to do that.

The cheering is growing louder as I climb the steps to the stage. My dad is waiting in the wings, and I wave for him to come out for our bow. He is waving for me to take a bow alone, which I do, as quick as I can, before running over to him.

Dad is beaming. "You did it, bud," he yells over the cheers and now the chanting that's started up. I can hear my basketball team leading it. Dad picks me up in a big bear hug. Then, I see Jen running up to us. Mom is right behind her, wheeling Grandpa, who is beaming. We hug, all five of us.

Anthony, Lamar, Sal, and Drake come up to us, high fiving me, slapping me on the back.

"Really cool, dude!"

"You got some talent, bro!"

They are all talking at the same time.

I hug Lamar and thank him. I can't believe how good it all turned out.

Then I start to make out what the audience is chanting.

"Are they chanting Jayster?" I ask my dad, hoping no one else heard me. I wouldn't want to sound like an egomaniac.

"No," Dad chuckles and wraps his arm around my shoulder. "They're chanting Jay Star."

My heart starts beating a million miles a minute, but in a good way...the best way.

* * *

AFTER A FEW MORE SECONDS, Principal Evans is back at the mic making a few announcements and ending the show. She calls all the acts onto the stage for one last bow. Then, it's over and I stand there for a minute. *Nothing went wrong. No one heckled us.* I'm trying to take it all in when I spot Gini, again, walking off the stage with her troupe.

I move to try to catch up with her but I'm stopped in my tracks by Gracy, who walks up right then and stands in front of me. She's looks oddly flustered and is holding the origami dove in both hands like it's a fragile kitten or something. Anthony elbows me and I shoot him a glare.

"You were amazing!" Gracy says, smiling with her mouth full of braces. *Oh no*, I think. I hope everyone knows we're totally platonic, especially Gini!

"Thanks?" I say. "Well, you know, we've always been sorta like cousins, so…"

I notice, then, that a new girl is standing right behind Gracy. The new girl Sal had talked about is looking at me, too.

"Excuse me," she says, softly, tapping Gracy on the shoulder. Gracy scowls at her (*I mean, she doesn't even try to hide it*) and steps away. Now, the new girl is standing right in front of me.

"Hi, I'm Miranda. I just moved here from Seattle and wanted to say that if you ever branch out totally on your own, you know, like, without your dad… what I'm saying is if you ever need a magician's assistant, let me know. I'm really into poi and I started juggling recently, too. I'd totally love to audition."

I notice Anthony then, standing behind her, raising his eyebrows up and down. I don't know what to say.

"OK, that sounds good," I spit out.

Miranda says, "Cool."

My head is buzzing. I don't even notice that my dad has walked over. He looks a bit shell-shocked, too.

"You know what I think," Dad says, "I think, after basketball season ends, we should try out for America's Got Talent! I mean, the whole school was chanting 'Jay Star.' How neat is that?"

"Is that what everyone calls you?" Miranda asks me.

"Nah, that's the first time anyone has ever called me that," I tell her. "Just call me Jay."

I stick out my hand and we shake. She gives me a flirty smile and walks away.

We stand there, my dad's arm around my shoulder, looking out at the crowd emptying out of the auditorium. If this is what Dad meant by adapting, I'm in.

I so totally got this.

ACKNOWLEDGMENTS

When you have been working toward the goal of publishing a novel for over 20 years, you have a lot of people to thank! My journey with writing started in fifth grade when I wrote my first short story. I remember how excited I was to show that story to my older sisters, Deb Sefton and Laura Rein, who have been hugely inspiring to me in so many ways, particularly through their love of literature and art. I cannot count the number of times I've turned to them for writing advice and support over the years. Thank you both for being my first readers and best friends.

I'm grateful for my brothers Jimmy and David Olson, my in-laws, Tom Rein, Shyrll and Cindy Olson, Melissa Cunningham, and my entire family for loving me through this entire journey. Huge thanks to my cousin, Lynn VanderLinde, who has been an amazing beta reader, offering her expert revisions, critique, and so much more. I would not have published this novel if it were not for Lynn's constant encouragement.

Fifth Avenue Press is a unique, author-centric endeavor managed by librarians (who we all know ROCK!). They do this work because they want to see more local authors succeed in the publishing world. The entire concept of Fifth Avenue Press is altruistic, from start to finish. I'm incredibly grateful to Fifth Avenue Press Editor Erin Helmrich who gave me a chance and has selflessly guided me through the daunting publishing process. She found the awesome book cover artist Jenny Zemanek, whose work perfectly fit my novel, and hired

Michelle Giorlando to serve as my editor. Michele, thank you for gifting me with your clear insights during the development and copy-editing phases. And thank you Nate Pocsi-Morrison for your excellent design work and advice.

Middle School is No Place for Magic was inspired by a magic show my husband and I took my daughter to years ago. During the show, I noticed that the magician's son was performing as his assistant. He looked to be about 10, near my daughter's age at that time. As with most stories, this one started with a "what if." *What if I had grown up with a magician for a dad?* Then, I thought back to the intense levels of embarrassment I frequently felt during those trepidatious middle school years and wondered what life will be like for the magician's son as he grew older. That is how this book came to be.

About midway through the novel, I decided to seek out a local magician to consult on the novel. That very week in a café, I spotted a card tacked to a bulletin board for Boyer the Magic Guy. I called Jeff Boyer, who invited me to come and see his show. It wasn't until after we sat down for a chat that I realized Jeff was the magician at that show so many years ago – the inspiration for my novel! We have been collaborating ever since.

I am thankful for Jeff's friendship, guidance, stories, and willingness to partner with me on future book tours. Through Jeff, I met Rick Fisher from FAB Magic of Vicksburg, Michigan, who has also been incredibly generous with his advice and time. Thank you for sharing your immense passion for magic with me and for partnering to create a magic trick box to go along with this novel.

In the spring of 2020, I was honored to work with award-winning poet Zilka Joseph who skillfully revised the two poems included in this novel, "The Dig" and "Of All the Things." I also want to thank Author Shirin Yim Leos who provided a critique that was not only insightful but motivating. Her encouragement helped push me forward at a time when I was feeling discouraged.

I have been so fortunate along my journey to have developed fruitful and lasting relationships with many individuals in the Ann Arbor/Detroit writing community. Through this journey, many in my writing community have grown into dear friends and I am grateful for each of them.

My late parents, Nancy and Frank Olson, raised me and my siblings to keep an open mind, follow our passions, and try new things just for the fun of it. My dad was one of the best storytellers I've ever known. For various reasons, including having a sweet younger sister (my Aunt Kathryn) who was happy to read to him, he didn't bother learning until he was seven. After he started reading, he never stopped, carrying a paperback in his pocket everywhere he went. My mom instilled a deep respect for teachers and librarians in us, and one of the best things she ever did for me was to sign me up for the Scholastic Book Club. It was so exciting to get new books right in the mail! Both parents provided us with the kind of childhood in which our imaginations could run wild. I count that as one of my biggest blessings.

To Steve, my college sweetheart, my husband, and my best friend - thank you. You have supported me, cheered for me, held me tight, and encouraged me ALL these years. Thank you for being a constant source of joy.

Lastly, I want to recognize my daughter, Leah, for the hours and hours you've spent in your 19 years brainstorming story ideas, reading drafts, and offering advice to inform my work. You are an incredible storyteller and artist. More than that, you have the most beautiful heart. I am the luckiest person in the world to be your mom.

ABOUT THE AUTHOR

Mimi Olson has been writing professionally for over 30 years, starting in high school with a sports reporting gig at a local newspaper. Publications include pieces in *Metro Parent, Jack and Jill, High Five Magazine, Pulse* and *Highlights*. She lives in Ann Arbor with her husband, daughter, and two very spoiled cats. *Middle School is No Place for Magic* is her debut novel.

Printed in the USA
CPSIA information can be obtained
at www.ICGtesting.com
LVHW032129200923
758623LV00012B/1253